PRINCESS OF AMINABAD

An Ordinary Life

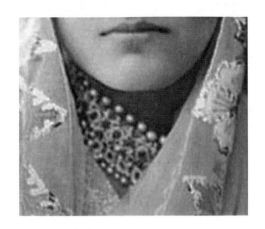

PRINCESS OF AMINABAD
An Ordinary Life

SUDHIR JAIN

BAYEUX ARTS
DIGITAL-TRADITIONAL PUBLISHING

Copyright Bayeux Arts 2014

Publication: July 2014

The author wishes to thank Sarah Jain, Barb Howard, Pat Kover and Brigid Stewart for their editorial help.

This is a work of fiction. Any correspondence with individuals or particular incidents is coincidental.

www.bayeux.com

Cover and Book design: PreMediaGlobal

All comments in the text are the author's own, and do not reflect the views of the Publishers.

Library and Archives Canada Cataloguing in Publication

Jain, Sudhir, 1938–, author
    Princess of Aminabad : an ordinary life / Sudhir Jain.

ISBN 978-1-897411-79-7 (pbk.)

    I. Title.

PS8619.A369P75 2014   C813'.6   C2014-900466-4

Printed in Canada

The ongoing publishing activities of Bayeux Arts, under its "Bayeux" and "Gondolier" imprints, are supported by the Canada Council for the Arts, the Government of Alberta, Alberta Multimedia Development Fund, and the Government of Canada through the Book Publishing Industry Development Program.

Canada Council for the Arts   Conseil des Arts du Canada

Alberta Culture

LIVRES CANADA BOOKS

DEDICATION

*Dedicated to my life partner Evelyn
who makes it all worthwhile.*

AUTHOR'S NOTES

The events take place in North India in and around Delhi. The language of conversation is Hindi and the dialogue is intended to convey some of the original flavour. The India of the period was a combination of current India, Pakistan and Bangladesh. It was part of British Empire. The population of three hundred millions consisted of Hindus (75 percent), Muslims (20 percent) and Christians (5%). The actors in this story are mostly Hindus. The five thousand year old religion had various sects, some of which began as reform movements at different periods of history. Jainism is one such sect founded by Lord Mahavir around twenty four hundred years ago.

Hindus of twentieth century were (and to a lesser extent still are) hostages to a strict caste system. Brahmins are the priests and the most revered, followed by the warrior class, business groups and untouchables in that order. While the crossover in the top three classes has been fairly common throughout history, untouchables were forced to stay in the lowly jobs of cleaning latrines, disposing of human waste and animal corpses till fifty years ago. They were not allowed to share the public services like wells and had to beg for water and other necessities for their survival. Many of them were beginning to convert to Islam in the early 1920s.

Wives in those days did not refer to their husbands by name. That tradition has been honoured in the dialogues.

THE CHARACTERS

Ramdas, *a middle-class farmer*
Kammo Bibi, *his wife*
Sarla and Kanaka, *their daughters*
Satto and Suraj, *their sons*
Panditji, *generic title for the holy man of the community*
Kanwar Sen, *a rich man in Ashapur*
Umrao Singh, *a prominent landlord in Aminabad*
Shivanand, *son of Kanwar Sen*
Gomti, *daughter of Kanwar Sen*
Raj Singh, *son of Umrao Singh*
Devi, *daughter of Umrao Singh*
Komal, *Devi's husband*
Kiran, *their daughter*
(Lord) Mahavir, *one of the messengers of God who founded Jainism, a Hindu sect*
Bina, *wife of Suraj*
Nirmala, *daughter of Kanaka and Raj Singh*
Padma, *daughter of Bina and Suraj*
Paramesh, Vijay and Rajneesh, *sons of Sarla and Shivanand*
Banwari Lal, *husband of Gomti*
Yagni and Ganesh, *sons of Gomti and Banwari Lal*
Parvati, *daughter of Gomti and Banwari Lal*
Santosh, Satya, Ravi and Rishi, *sons of Nirmala and Ganesh*
Munimji, *accountant of Shivanand*
Monica, *a young white girl.*
Servants, *relatives and friends.*

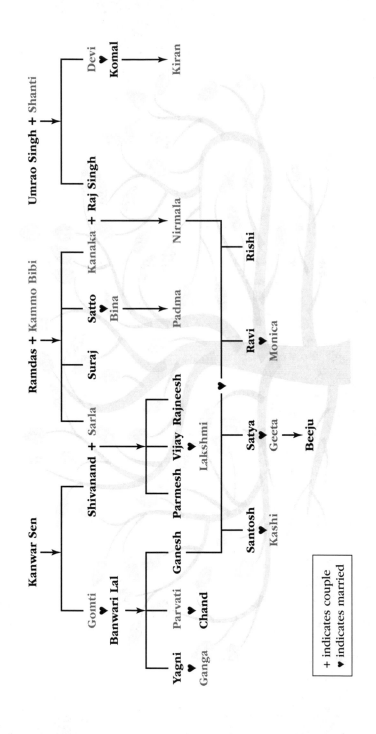

LIST OF HINDI WORDS

Arey	Hey
Ayurvedic	Traditional Indian
Avatar	Incarnation
Bahu	Daughter-in-law
Bas	Enough
Beta	Son
Bhabi	Sister
Bhagwan	God
Bhaiya	Brother
Bitiya	Dear daughter
Bua	Father's sister
Chacha	Father's brother
Dharmshala	Lodging attached to a temple
Devar	Younger brother of husband
Dhoti	A cotton sheet worn around and across the legs
Gora, gori, gorey	White man, woman, people
Hai	An expression of grief
Jai	Victory
Jalebi	A sweet dish popular with breakfast on a special occasion.
Ji	Honorific suffix
Ji han	Yes sir/madam
Jija	Husband of sister
Jiji	Sister
Kheer	Rice pudding
Khush raho	Joy be with you

Lahanga	*Colourful full skirt*
Lassi	*A buttermilk drink*
Mahavir	*One of the founders of Jainism*
Mama	*Mother's brother*
Mausi	*Mother's sister*
Mem	*White woman of rank*
Nana	*Mother's father*
Nani	*Mother's mother*
Pahari	*Migrant(s) from mountains*
Pandit	*Person offering religious services*
Panjiri, Sandesh	*Fudge with ground nuts*
Paplu	*A card game for three players, a version of Rummy.*
Paratha	*A type of chapati*
Pita	*Father*
Ras Malai	*Cheese balls in cream with sugar*
Sabka Gulam	*Servant of all*
Sahib	*An honorific for white and brown officers in colonial days*
Sanyasi, sanyasin	*A wandering monk, male, female*
Sari	*Long wrap-around outerwear used, draped around, by many Indian women*
Takhat	*A wood platform the size of a double bed*

The Princess of Aminabad used up every drop of her energy in accomplishing the goal the times she lived in had set for her.

1
Childhood

(1905–1932)

*Y*ears 1905–1918: The giant asleep since the British rulers crushed the Mutiny of 1857 was waking up. Mohandas Karamchand Gandhi had returned from South Africa. The Indian National Congress and the Muslim League were working together, campaigning for Indian self-government. However, when World War One started in Europe, barring some exceptions like Netaji Subhas Chandra Bose, Gandhi and many other politicians, Maharajahs, and wealthy and ordinary people provided support, some by donating money, others volunteering for the army. 800,000 Indian soldiers fought in Europe; 50,000 did not return. While Indian soldiers sacrificed their lives in Europe and North Africa, Gandhi led movements which ended indentured labour and Indigo plantations in Bihar, establishing his stature as Mahatma (saint) and Bapu (father) among the masses. The British rulers drained India of every rupee they could find and the country was almost bankrupt at the end of the war.

1

If Ramdas had known how the day would turn out, he would not have been so pensive this fine spring morning. The glow of the crimson sun behind the blossoming mango trees at the far end of his farm warmed the air and should have been pleasant after a cool night, but it was not. Ramdas looked into the distance, across the flat land and wondered what was at the end of the earth. If only his eyes were strong enough to see that far. The only sound was the twittering of the parrots in the distance; the rest of the family and the servants were not awake yet.

Ramdas had a hundred acres which he farmed himself. The land was fertile and yielded bountiful harvests of wheat, sugarcane and barley most years. He worked hard, respected those to whom respect was due and treated workers with fairness. He had earned his good name in the community. Which was just as well because, before long, suitable grooms would have to be found for his two daughters. He wanted his sons, Satto and Suraj, to get a good education and work for the Raj where opportunities to make money without breaking your back were many. Therefore, even though the boys were only twelve and nine years old, he sent them both to boarding schools in Saharanpur, twenty miles away. They came home every weekend and on holidays. Amazing how good the city air was for them, Satto was already almost as tall as Ramdas and still growing.

The village of Songaon had about fifty mud huts with thatched roofs. A hut had two or three rooms for all members of the family as well as the animals in inclement weather. The only brick house in the village was built by Ramdas soon after he took over the farm from his aging father. The house was built around a courtyard, two rooms on each side. Rooms in

the front of the house opened outside on to a covered verandah and the farm. Other rooms faced the courtyard. Rooms
on one side were used as the kitchen and the store room.
Rooms on the other sides were used for normal living during
the day and for sleeping at night. There was a hand pump
in the centre of the courtyard for water for general use and
another in the kitchen for cooking. Ramdas employed three
or four servants, at different times, to run the household and
scores of labourers on the farm.

Most of the residents were Hindus of various sects who
lived in harmony. Ramdas and other men in the village wore
loose cotton shirts and dhoti. They were a couple of inches
taller than five feet, their skin tanned to dark brown. Even
the older men had full head of black hair and every one
had dark eyes. The women were a few inches shorter than
men, wore cotton saris and blouses and tended to gain size
after childbearing. They used the end of sari to cover their
heads in public, a few covered their faces as well. In cold
weather, both men and women wrapped wool shawls around
their upper bodies. It was easy to separate poor, working
men and women from those in comfortable circumstances.
Poor people were generally shorter, their skin darker, bodies
skinnier. They washed themselves and their clothes rarely,
went around in bare feet and assumed a subservient air when
their betters were nearby even when there was no dealing
between them.

As the sun rose this morning, Ramdas was strolling on the
verandah from one end to the other chewing on the neem
twig which was his tooth brush and toothpaste in one. He
was wondering how long the good times would last. For as
long as he could remember the Raj was firmly entrenched.
Gorey Sahibs treated honest people fairly and crooks firmly.

People knew their place and stayed there. Muslims lived in their communities without bothering the Hindus and whatever interaction there was, it was conducted in a civil manner. The different castes did what was expected of them; women stayed behind the screen in their homes, young respected the old, and the Sahibs did not meddle with the social customs of the natives. But Ramdas had a suspicion it could not last; good times never do.

The juice was now chewed out of the twig. He washed his mouth with water from the jug, threw some water on his face and called Bhola. It was time for his morning tea and to get ready to assign work for the labourers. No point worrying about the future; he couldn't do anything about it anyway.

It was nearly noon when Panditji dropped by on one of the regular visits he made to check up on the well being of his faithfuls. Panditji was the priest in the village temple and he conducted all religious ceremonies from birth to death. He considered participating in the joys and sorrows of the members of his flock his prime duty and took a keen interest in their affairs. He knew when the children were ready to marry and helped in locating suitable mates for them.

After the customary snack of paratha and panjiri helped down with a glass of butter milk spiced with salt and pepper, Panditji washed his hands and mouth. Ramdas thanked him for dropping by and, just as he was about to leave to check the workers, Panditji's words stopped him, "I have some good news for you. Sit down and listen."

Ramdas replied, "I have felt low-spirited all morning. What kind of good news can there be today."

"I said good news; it is actually a great news. I've got two suitable boys for your Sarla. She will be eleven in a few weeks. Time to get her hitched. You won't find better boys than these. You can choose from one in the north in Ashapur or the one in the south in Aminabad."

"Who are the families you are talking of?"

"I am surprised you did not guess from my tone. Surely you know Kanwar Sen of Ashapur and Umrao Singh of Aminabad."

"Panditji, stop making fun of me. Kanwar Sen and Umrao Singh are great families and I am a poor farmer. I could not match their expectations if I sold myself as a slave. Or are you thinking of families I am not aware of?"

"Arey, arey, Ramdas, when have I made fun of you? A month ago Sevakji dropped by the temple on his way to bathe in Ganga in Haridwar. You know him; he serves Lord Mahavir in the temple Kanwar Sen built. He was asking about Sarla in great detail. Kanwar Sen wants a good girl from a decent family for his oldest son Shivanand; he doesn't need a big dowry. He wants to settle the matter soon though. Sivanand is going to England for two years to qualify as a barrister and you can't send a son across seven seas without tying the knot first."

"Why did you keep it a secret from me for a month?'

"I was waiting for confirmation which I got this morning. But I have to tell you more. Metharam, munshi of Umrao Singh of Aminabad came for puja on his way to Saharanpur. Umrao Singh wants to know all about Sarla too."

"Panditji, do you know why these great families are interested in my daughter? What do we have that thousands of families don't?"

"Ramdas, you are renowned as an honest, God serving man. You will add honour to any family. Don't be so humble for your daughter's sake. Give me your word to follow up and I will do what is needed."

"Let me think about it for a couple of days. Sarla can't marry both boys and she is too young to choose."

"You might consider Umrao Singh for Kanaka. Raj Singh is only twelve. They might agree to wait a year or two till your baby daughter is ready."

"That is an idea. Let me think about it too."

"Think for a few days but do not take too long. Kanwar Sen won't wait.

On his way out Bhola handed Panditji an earthen pot. Panditji looked into it, saw it was full of sweets and savoury snacks, thanked Bhola and muttered a blessing for Ramdas. Panditji would have blessed Ramdas even if he did not shower him with gifts on every visit; Pandjiti was able to find suitable life partners for young ones and this had given him the feeling that all was well in this world.

2

Kammo Bibi heard the conversation from behind the bamboo curtain which let in the light and protected her from the flies and evil eyes of male visitors. As soon as the holy man departed she called her husband,

"Are you going to tell me what you are going to do to my daughters or will I learn it from servants' gossip?'

"Kammo dear, I am in shock. It came like the bolt of lightning that killed our best cow last fall. The girls are still growing; I thought we could wait a couple of years before looking for grooms."

"You go round with your eyes closed and whatever I say never enters your head. I was younger than Sarla before our engagement. I mentioned that to you only last week. Now Panditji says it and lightning strikes you. 'Let me think about it.' What is there to think? Do you want your daughters to go to great families or hand them over to urchins no one wants?"

"Be patient, Kammo. It doesn't look good to rush into these things. I will tell Panditji on Tuesday to get the horoscopes of the boys and tell us the best pairing. We don't want to start this process on a Friday. You know that Friday always brings bad luck."

"If you want to insult Kanwar Sen and Umrao Singh by waiting for four days go ahead. If what I am fearing really happens, I will remind you till my dying day that your Kammo told you not to wait."

"Kammo, don't be angry. You are right. There is no need to wait."

Ramdas conceded defeat. He sent Bhola to fetch Panditji who came running and asked as soon as he got his breath, "Ramdas, have you decided already?"

"Before we decide we need to check that the planets are in their proper places. Can you get their horoscopes and confirm the match?"

"Ramdas don't be a fool. Their horoscopes were made by their priests and I can not be certain of their accuracy. I will get the exact times of the birth of the boys and make new horoscopes. Then we will know how well or poorly they match."

"It will take you a month or two to do all this. Will they wait?"

"Once they know you are interested they will wait. You are not asking for anything unusual. Every father with a child's interest in his heart would do the same. Ramdas, think for a moment. Why would a good family want a girl whose father is impatient to unload her?"

The days went by slowly. Panditji's visits stopped altogether. Kammo asked her husband almost every day whether he had heard anything and his replies were beginning to show some irritation. It was nearly noon on a Tuesday four weeks later when Panditji showed up all smiles.

"Stars of Shivanand and Sarla are almost aligned. The horoscopes are not a perfect match but they never are. I do not think a slight divergence should worry us."

Ramdas was pleased. "If it does not worry you, I am not going to lose sleep over it either. Now what about the other two? I want Raj Singh in the family too."

"The horoscopes of Raj Singh and Kanaka do not agree either but, again, the divergence is not that great. There are many couples with worse horoscopes who live happily with many sons and hardly any daughters. Planets foretell a long prosperous life for Raj Singh and many boys for the couple. What more can one wish?"

Kammo Bibi, watching the proceedings from behind the bamboo curtain as usual, could not contain herself, "This is wonderful. Panditji, when can you go to Ashapur and Aminabad to settle the matters?"

"I can go whenever it suits you. Hari Ram can look after the temple for the week I will be away."

Panditji visited both families and presented them with a coconut, a brass pot of pure ghee, an earthen lamp and a hundred and one silver rupees as the opening salvo in marriage negotiations. He returned with red glass bangles, a silk sari and gold anklets from each of his visits as signs of provisional acceptance. The ladies from the two households dropped by. Kammo Bibi called the girls the day before their arrival, made them stand side by side in front of her and said in a very serious tone, "Some ladies are visiting to meet with you. It is very important that you make a nice impression on them. You must wash your faces and put on clean clothes I give you. I will put mustard oil in your hair and arrange it nicely before they come and don't mess it up. When they speak to you, answer them but very softly. Do not make remarks or ask questions; speak only when you are spoken to." The girls suppressed their giggles through the lecture and followed the instructions to the letter. They knew something of great importance was afoot although they had no inkling of what it could be. The visitors were satisfied that the girls were of fair complexion, soft spoken and thin but healthy. All was now set for the priests to name the auspicious dates for Sagai—formal confirmation of marriage plans, Sarla in October two days before Diwali, festival of Lakshmi, the goddess of wealth, and Kanaka a week after the joyous spring festival of Holi the following April.

The Sagai ceremonies were simple affairs. Ramdas and Kammo Bibi traveled to each groom's home in an ox cart. The family priest started prayers at the appointed minute and chanted mantras throughout the ceremony and told the parents when to repeat particular prayers after him. At appropriate moments the priest prompted Ramdas to present the prospective groom and the father English wool for Achkans for cool winter evenings, and mothers and sisters with fine cotton saris. They received, in return, rings and saris for the brides. The girls stayed home, not realizing that their future was being decided without their knowledge, let alone consent. They did learn of their good fortunes in appropriate detail from Kammo Bibi after her return.

The priests of all three families re-examined the horoscopes to set the auspicious dates and decided that Sarla was to be married to Shivanand next spring, and Kanaka to Raj Singh in the autumn two years later. Preparations started for Sarla's wedding straight away. Saris were ordered several months in advance; tailors camped on the verandah for weeks sewing cholis for the women and kurtas, achkans and trousers for men. Jewellers came from Benares to take measurements of wrists, necks, waists, fingers, ankles and toes to make sure ornaments fit properly. Kammo Bibi determined what kinds of saris and jewels were to accompany her daughters so that they were treated with respect in their new homes. Ramdas accepted her demands with equanimity because he was elated at being accepted by families of such high stature. Even though a dowry was not demanded by either groom, Ramdas negotiated a mortgage on the farm with the local moneylender to pay for celebrations which would be appropriate to the station of the grooms. Two weeks before Sarla's wedding day, guests started arriving from far and wide. Two large tents were set up to accommodate them along with a kitchen tent with wood stoves and a large collection of metal plates and bowls. Four cooks worked non-stop from morning till night to keep the guests' gastronomic juices flowing.

Ladies from the groom's family arrived en masse the day before the wedding. Somehow every one was accommodated and no one minded the inconvenience of overcrowding. Sarla was surrounded by older ladies who made beautiful designs on her face, hands and feet with henna paste that left pinkish red stains after it dried. Her clothes and jewels were tried one more time. Then the ladies of all ages assembled in the courtyard where men were not allowed and took turns singing and dancing. The jolly evening lasted almost till dawn.

On the day of the wedding, the groom's party of two hundred men arrived in the late afternoon on carts pulled by horses or oxen. At the entrance of the village, men arranged themselves in a long procession led by Shivanand on a white steed. Although it was quite hot, the groom was dressed in white, tight cotton pants and pale blue achkan which was extensively decorated with gold threads and semiprecious stones. On his head was a similarly adorned turban with a long thick tail. Brothers of the groom dressed in similar splendour and rode at his sides. Men in the family followed in order of seniority, some on horses, many on foot. Ramdas received the procession and led them to a large tent that had been erected for the purpose. Servants in white kurtas and pajamas appeared from nowhere and led the horses to the makeshift stable some distance away. After courteous introductions, guests attacked the delectable dishes as fast as the servants could bring them.

Just before sunset, the servants brought in kerosene lamps and placed them on small tables along the walls of the tent. Panditji had determined from the horoscopes that the hour of seven was especially auspicious for the ceremony. A few minutes before this hour, Sarla was led in by Satto, her older brother. One end of her gold embroidered red sari was pulled over to act as a veil and protect her from evil glances. Gold ornaments studded with diamonds, rubies and emeralds covered her from head to toe. Ramdas gently took her right hand in his left as she entered the tent and they walked slowly to the fire in the far corner where Panditji was chanting mantras and feeding the flames with ghee. The groom, his face also veiled but only partially, was led by his father to face the bride. The bride and groom, two children, sat opposite each other looking at the ground with smiling faces. Not one word was exchanged between the two who had never seen each other and yet were happily going through with a ceremony which would unite them for eternity, if mantras were to have their effect. After a few minutes of prayer, Panditji asked them to stand up. He picked up a rolled silk sheet about two feet in length, gave one end of it to the groom and the other to the bride. The couple went round the fire seven times, the bride following the groom while Panditji chanted prayers for the long fruitful marriage with many sons and few hardships. After these rounds, the couple sat down side by side facing the holy fire and across from Panditji who talked to them gently and amicably about the responsibilities they had to each other and to their families. This was followed by blessings from the family and friends who came one by one, touched them on the head, said a few words of advice and dropped rupee notes in the lap of the bride. The couple looked amused at first but the smiles disappeared after a while and then they took turns yawning. Eventually, the bride nodded off and the groom started rubbing his eyes, Experienced Panditji was looking for this signal, He nodded to the parents and the couple were taken inside the house where they were fed and put to bed in separate rooms.

The party had come to an end. The ladies were accommodated inside the rather crowded house. Men found space where they could, on the verandah or under the tent, spread the bedrolls they had brought with them and slept soundly not bothered by the hard ground. Most of them woke up fresh and exchanged smiles or jokes with servants serving steaming sweet chai in earthen mugs. After a simple breakfast of buttermilk and parathas they walked in small groups to their carts. The groom and his immediate family stayed for another week for celebrations on a smaller scale.

Soon after Sarla's wedding, preparations started for that of Kanaka. It was a similar affair. People were conventional in those days and followed a set routine for important events. Kammo was happy that great families had accepted her daughters. Ramdas was relieved that there was no untoward incident and expenses were a little less than he had feared they would be. Satto and Suraj had worked hard during the weddings and were glad they were over.

———◊◊———

It was customary that the bride stayed at her parents' home till she was at least fourteen. However, the bride's life changed altogether. She was no longer a carefree child; she was a married girl preparing for life in a new home with responsibilities to shoulder. Gone were mid-morning lessons from the Guruji who was as old as the banyan tree in the yard—his back bent, a long white beard and a few strands of hair on his head. He always wore a crumpled but clean saffron robe and carried a stick to lean on. He often threatened to use it on their behind if the girls misbehaved but never actually did. Academic education for girls was considered a waste of time and money once they could read and write and knew the elementary rudiments of arithmetic. There were no more visits to the cousins, teasing other kids or rope skipping. The fun was replaced by a mixture of joyful anticipation of a married life and dread of an unknown future. Their days were all about preparing for life in a new home with the new family, learning the skills they needed to run a household: cooking, embroidery, knitting and, the most important, following their mother's detailed instructions on how to show respect to the in-laws.

Sarla stayed home till she was sixteen and moved to Ashapur only when Shivanand returned from England. The dates of the Farewell Ceremony were set a week before harvest festival by the priest of receiving family. Satto accompanied Sarla to Ashapur. Sarla dressed in a red sari and minimal jewelry because most it had already gone with Kanwar Sen after the wedding to be displayed in Ashapur. There were bucketful of tears shed by Kammo Bibi, Sarla and other female relatives who were visiting for the occasion. Even stoic Ramdas had moist eyes. Sarla bowed before every older relative and touched their feet before being helped on to the Ox cart by Ramdas. The cart was padded with extra mattresses for the long journey. Suraj sat facing Sarla with the cases of clothes and a package of food for the journey between them. Every one shouted Hare Ram in unison as the cart pulled off. Panditji stopped chanting after the cart had gone out of sight and joined the rest for a soothing drink of lassi and sweet snacks. In view of the relative youth of Kanaka and Raj, it was a couple of years later when Kanaka left for Aminabad chaperoned by Suraj.

Three years after his return Shivanand lost most of his hearing after an illness and had to give up the lucrative practice of law. However, he turned a tragedy into triumph. He took over the management of the family property and succeeded in growing it manifold. He became the most prominent citizen of Ashapur and was the owner of the first motor vehicle there, a Crossley touring car. He was equally at home with Congress leaders visiting the town to lead the protest movement and the local British rulers who were determined to squelch it. One week Nehru would be his house guest and the next week the Governor of the province slept in the same sheets, albeit washed and immaculately ironed, and would be attended by the same servants. For all appearances Sarla was happy even though Shivanand took another wife who was kept discreetly in a separate bungalow.

3

Aminabad was a small town of about four thousand people. The population was evenly divided among Hindus and Muslims who had split the town into two distinct areas and lived peacefully in them. Each section had its own shops; contact between the two groups was limited to essential professional services like the doctor who was a Hindu or the lawyer who was a Muslim. A huge dome and the four minarets of the mosque dominated the homes in Muslim area. The Hindu area had nothing so grand but the homes were larger and less crowded. Each sect had its own rather unpretentious temple. The Jain temple, where Umarao prayed on every Tuesday was perhaps the most austere, as suited the simple living movement founded more than two thousand years ago. Austerity did not extend to the personal living of the followers, however, and the largest structure in the town was the home of Umrao Singh. Umrao owned several thousand acres, some farmed by him and some by the tenant farmers. Unlike most others of that era, Umrao was a generous landlord and treated the tenants kindly, even forgiving their dues in years of drought.

A week after the harvest festival of Diwali, heat of the summer was gone and cold of the winter still a month away. It was a warm sunny November day when Kanaka and Suraj traveled the distance of thirty miles for twelve hours from Songaon to Aminabad in a horse cart. She was tired but also excited about the new life opening up for her. At the entrance of the town she was transferred to a plush palaki carried on the shoulders of four strong men. Suraj walked stiffly along the palaki angrily waving away the curious gawkers. The curtains intended to hide her from the curious onlookers jiggled with the movement allowing her to peek at the surroundings. As she went through the market street which was much grander than that of her village, her heart started beating faster and she clasped her hands around her knees tighter and tighter. Then the palaki turned into a small quiet street and she noticed a high brick wall with a gate big enough to let a mounted elephant through. She was carried past a uniformed guard standing at attention with a sword hanging from his belt, and then she entered a large yard covered with bricks. Her palaki swung to the right and went past a platform through a hallway into the courtyard. The assembly of women of all ages stopped chattering as the palaki entered. The men put the palaki to the floor, bowed and quietly slipped away. Suraj raised the curtain and helped his sister out. Kanaka was greeted by the beaming face of Shanti, her mother-in-law. Kanaka had rehearsed this moment hundreds of times. She wrapped the loose end of sari round her waist, bent down and touched Shanti's feet. Shanti pulled her up and hugged her. The process was repeated with her sister-in-law Devi and dozens of other relatives and older lady visitors from the village.

At last the dinner was served. Kanaka was so tired by then that she dozed off in between the courses. Devi took her upstairs to one of the two rooms the couple was to occupy and helped her to bed. Raj Singh came after the ladies had gone to sleep, found his bride soundly asleep, slept on his own cot and went out in the morning without Kanaka noticing him. But she did welcome the stranger as her lord and master the next night. As time passed, each grew fond of the other. Getting to know each other intimately was a slow process, and not very important to them. Men and women lived in spheres which did not overlap much.

Kanaka had been trained well and she found the change in her life quite pleasant. Umrao and Raj spent their days managing the estate and the evenings on the brick platform in front of the main house. The household was run by Shanti who made sure that the maids and servants did the jobs she assigned to them properly and on time. Kanaka had no responsibilities to speak of. She would have been bored stiff if it were not for her sister-in-law. Devi lived with her husband and a one-year old boy in a small house in the compound but detached from the main building. Komal, her husband, owned a dry good store on the main street where he attended to the customers from morning till dark. He supplemented the income from the store by lending small sums to needy customers at a reasonable rate of interest. He was a proud man, very conscious of his relatively low position and stayed out as much as possible from Umrao household. Kanaka spent part of most mornings with Devi helping her in looking after the boy. Devi introduced Kanaka to women in the village who were only a little below their status and who could be socialized with.

The winters were mild, summers not two hot and crops good. Kanaka settled down to a life of luxury to which she was not accustomed. Shanti showed her great consideration and it helped. Two years passed uneventfully. It was autumn again. The monsoon was over and skies blue spotted only by parrots, crows, chickadees and pigeons. The preparations were in full swing for the Dusshera, the harvest festival when family and friends visited each other and shared their good fortunes. One afternoon when they were preparing snacks for the visitors, Devi noticed that Kanaka was not her normal chirpy self and pointed this out to her mother. Shanti felt Kanaka's head, asked her some questions and sent for the midwife. She pronounced Kanaka pregnant, to every one's delight. From then till the birth there was never a day when a Brahmin did not come to chant long prayers for the baby to be a boy and did not return home with sacks of flour and lentils. Devi too became pregnant soon with her second baby but it was not a source of excitement in the household. It did not bother Devi because she knew her position in the family as a daughter. The two girls did have a better time going through the pregnancy together than they would have had otherwise.

Umrao insisted that the convention of a mother returning to her parents for the birth of her first child would not be followed. Much to the general disappointment the baby was not the boy. However, the baby girl was healthy and had a fair complexion. Panditji threw rice and water from holy river Ganges over her body while naming her Nirmala, the pure one. She soon became the apple of everyone's eye. After all, there was plenty of time to have sons.

Devi also gave birth to a girl a week later. She called her Kiran, ray of light.

Year 1918: The Great War was over and victorious England was celebrating. However, there was no joy in India. The general expectation that the country would be rewarded by self-rule after the war was not met. There was a feeling of being let down all over the country, made worse by an influenza epidemic which killed six million people in two years. Repressive laws were passed. Mahatma Gandhi started his first peaceful protest, later known as satyagraha, in India. The brutal suppression culminated on April 13, 1919 when Gen. Dyer ordered his soldiers to open fire on 2000 peaceful protesters in a walled compound in Jallianwala Bag near the Golden Temple in Amritsar, Punjab and killed 379 and seriously wounded 200 others in ten minutes. Gandhi now became the undisputed voice of the independence movement. Unfortunately, the British succeeded in sowing seeds of suspicion towards the Hindu majority in Jinnah, most prominent among the Muslim leaders.

The misery of unusually cold winter continued into spring. Spring is normally a dry season in but this year it rained almost every afternoon. A downpour caught Raj when he was returning home after supervising the seeding of wheat. After he had changed into dry clothes Kanaka brought him a thali with a tumbler of hot milk and some jalebis. He waved her aside, saying, "Take it away. I do not feel hungry." She noticed that he was shivering. She put her palm on his forehead. The hot touch alarmed her. She made him lie on the bed and covered him with a blanket. After making sure he was comfortable, she sent the servant to Shanti and Umrao to report Raj's condition.

Soon, a local Ayurvedic pundit rushed in and prescribed a mixture of herbs. Shanti and Kanaka sat next to the bed, Shanti putting cold compress on Raj's forehead, Kanaka massaging his feet. Umrao sat in a chair next to the wall and watched anxiously. Raj did not sleep all night and kept muttering meaningless sentences. His condition was worse in the morning and the Western doctor was called in. He examined the patient, nodded sagely, took out two bottles from his bag and explained that the powder was to be given with water every four hours, the paste rubbed on his forehead every hour. On his way out he told Umrao, "It does not look good but there is still hope." To cover all angles, Umrao engaged holy men in saffron robes to chant mantras day and night. On most occasions, any one of these efforts would have borne fruit. But this time they failed altogether. Raj closed his eyes on the third day and his breathing stopped that night.

Kanaka became a widow at the age of nineteen. "I have nothing to live for. I am not going to live the life of a widow. I am not going to be a burden," she screamed running towards the flames of the burning sandalwood pyre consuming the body of Raj, her god on earth. Devi rushed forward, grabbed her and held her tightly around the waist in both her arms saying repeatedly, "You can't do that. You have Nirmala to think of. I won't let you leave a sweet two year old without a mother now that Mahavirji has taken her father away."

Umrao and Shanti were devastated by the death of their only son because they loved him. There were some practical considerations as well. Not only would he have looked after them in their old age, he would have chanted the appropriate couplets from scriptures in religious ceremonies at their death to make sure that their sins were forgiven and good deeds were enhanced in the eyes of gods.

Shanti had a solution for their problems. One afternoon when Umrao had just finished his lunch and was preparing for siesta, she said "You need someone trustworthy to look after the estate now that you are not young yourself. Devi and Kanaka are women; you need a man to do a man's jobs. Think about adopting Kanaka's brother Suraj as our son."

It took a few moments for the suggestion to sink in. Still scratching his head Umrao spoke as if talking to himself, "He is seventeen and seems to be a good boy. He will be better for Kanaka than some stranger taking over the estate." He smiled and added, "It is a great idea. I will tell Panditji to work it out."

Suraj and his family were delighted with this plan. Kanaka knew her brother well and had her doubts. But the opinion of the young widow was not sought because she was not expected to have an opinion, and Kanaka was too modest to express it to any one.

To get their minds off their grief, Shanti started to get Kanaka involved in running the household. She showed Kanaka the nitty gritty of management; ordering supplies, watching servants, keeping track of expenses and most important, how to satisfy Umrao's smallest wish even before he had expressed it. It took nearly a year before Shanti told Umrao one evening, "You don't need me any more. Kanaka can look after the household."

Umrao's face turned red, "Why do you have to say such silly things? Don't you know it is a bad omen? Just because Kanaka can tell servants what to do and when, you are not needed? I forbid you to think such things."

"I don't know about omens. All I know is that I don't want to live any more," Shanti replied. Her head was bowed, body tranquil.

Her wish was fulfilled the following Tuesday. On the way home from the temple after the evening prayers, Shanti told Kanaka of pain in her chest. Kanaka helped her lie down on the string bed in the courtyard. She closed her eyes and whispered "Mahavirji answered my prayers. I am going to see my Raju."

The death of his wife was a cruel blow. Umrao withdrew from the management of the estate altogether and left all decisions to young Suraj. Umrao reclined on a pillow on a takhat staring at an invisible object far away and refused to eat altogether. Kanaka, now wholly responsible for the family's well being, was shocked at the turn of events. When she talked to Suraj about him he threw his hands up and screamed, "What can I do about it? I have too much to do. It is harvest time. Talk to Munshiji and Panditji from the temple. They may have some ideas."

She sent a servant to ask Munshiji and Panditji to talk to Umrao. Munshiji had looked after family's finances since Umrao was a baby and Panditji had prayed for him when he was conceived and made his horoscope when he was borne. Both loved and admired him. They too had suffered the loss of loved ones and could understand his grief at losing an only son and then the wife in such a short period. Within an hour of receiving the message, they were sitting on either side of Umrao's feet on the takhat. Munshiji mentioned business matters which needed Umrao's consideration, more to attract his attention than to get his decision. But Umrao remained silent and unmoving. Then Panditji threw a stone in the dark, "You have to get out of your grief and take hold of yourself. You still have Suraj to look after. You have to get him settled with a wife before you give up." Panditji noticed a flicker in the eyes and continued, "What is even more important, the country is in the grip of communal conflicts. Your friendship with Maulana Rafi Ahmed is what keeps the peace in Aminabad. If you let yourself sink, the whole town might catch fire."

The arrows hit the mark. Umrao's gaze turned to Panditji, "You make good points. I do have responsibilities. I will meet with Maulana sahib when I am a little better. I also should get Suraj settled. Panditji, do you have someone in mind for him?"

"No, not at the moment. But I will send the word around. Suraj is a good boy and your name is worshipped in the community. We will soon be inundated with offers."

The visitors stood up, bowed deep with folded hands on their chest and left. Umrao called the servant and told him to bring him Lassi. When the servant informed Kanaka of the master's order she burst into a devotional song; her father-in-law was returning to his normal self.

Panditji spread the word on Suraj's eligibility but was shocked to receive no proposals. He had underestimated the impact of two recent deaths in the family on a superstitious community. He was alarmed at the responses he received. The respect for Umrao and his wealth was offset by the general belief that his family was cursed; one would have to be desperate to send their daughter to a house bedeviled by the messenger of death. The mothers of eligible girls had another suspicion. In the absence of a mother-in-law, Kanaka would order their daughter around and Suraj would not be able to defend his bride from his older sister.

Panditji was not a man to give up, not when his mentor depended on his success. His temple was founded by Umrao's father and it survived mainly on his largesse. Messengers were instructed to go farther out and be less discriminating in their search. A couple of weeks later he had three leads. One girl was fourteen and considered too old. Another was from a family where the father was known to drink too much too often. The third had six younger sisters and no brother, her family had a good name but little money. Bina could not read or write but, though only twelve, had been managing the household because her mother was ill more often than well.

Umrao and Devi visited the prospective bride. Devi would have liked the girl to be fair and a little thinner and Umrao would have preferred the family to have their own land and a more respectable home. However, Panditji was persuasive, "The girl has long lustrous black hair and expressive eyes and is very modest in speech. The family has a good reputation; they work hard and do not owe much to the moneylender. Her good points easily offset her minor shortcomings." Gifts of coconut and plain sari were exchanged and dates set for Sagai and the wedding within six months. The ceremony was a modest affair to suit the means of the bride's family; the groom's party was only fifty, the dowry was small and the celebrations lasted only three days. A year after the betrothal, Bina moved to her new home in Aminabad.

The discharge of his last familial responsibility returned Umrao to his depressed state. On Devi's suggestion Kanaka prepared his favourite dishes: pulao made with basmati rice specially brought in from Ashapur, cauliflower and spinach curries, stuffed potatoes, chick pea dal, halwah with cashew nuts and chapatis from maize flower covered with a thick layer of ghee. But he did nothing more than touch the food. He refused all prescriptions. Munshiji and Panditji failed in their attempts to make him feel better. All entreaties of Devi, Suraj and Kanaka fell on deaf ears. By the time the winter arrived he was mere skin and bones and stayed in bed all day. Then he caught a cold and passed away without a murmur one afternoon with Suraj, Bina and Kanaka beside his bed. Suraj did his part in all ceremonies reciting Sanskrit shlokas with great clarity. If it depended on his recitation alone, Umrao certainly attained Nirvana.

Devi and Kanaka were heart-broken. Kanaka's grief was worse because it was tinged with guilt. "In my five years here I have caused the death of every family member except you," she sobbed to her sister-in-law one afternoon when they got together. "I have brought a curse with me. You should keep away from me, you would not want the misfortune to land on you as well." Devi consoled her as much as she could and reminded her, "Don't be silly. Think of Nirmala. You are the only one she has. You have to get over this grief, for her sake if not yours."

"My poor baby! Who would care for her if something happens to me? I have to get over these feelings. You are right, I have to live for her." Kanaka replied, drying her tears.

Nirmala was now three and talked incessantly. Her playful entreaties, "Don't cry Amma, you don't look pretty with your eyes swollen," helped Kanaka recover some sense of normalcy. However, the toddler could do nothing to assuage the feeling of guilt.

———◊◊———

Bina was mature for her fourteen years and took over the household responsibilities during this period. Kanaka knew her position as a widow was precarious and did not attempt to take back control of the main household. Instead, she set up a separate kitchen for herself in her upstairs rooms.

It was a patriarchal society. Suraj inherited the property with the exception of a small acreage and some cash that farsighted Umrao had assigned to Kanaka. This provided her means to live in reasonable comfort and preserve the dowry she had brought with her to serve the same purpose for Nirmala. Devi, Umrao's only surviving child, knew that the dowry at her wedding was in lieu of share in the property and did not expect an inheritance. Suraj did not offer her any either even though he was aware of her difficult circumstances.

Nirmala was an energetic playful child. She spent a large part of her days at Devi's home playing with her two cousins, one two years older and other the same age as her. Bina also loved Nirmala and encouraged her to spend time with her downstairs. She did not see much of her husband; he was busy establishing his authority over the peasants. Suraj had a quick temper and a fear that if he showed any consideration he would be taken advantage of. His ruthlessness led to frequent quarrels and occasional violence and the arguments with neighbours were often settled in court. Thus, it was not long before Suraj had lost much of the goodwill he had inherited.

A year later Bina had a baby girl of her own. She stayed in Aminabad for the birth because her mother was expecting too. Kanaka and Devi looked after Bina when she needed caring. The baby was pretty and healthy and was named Padma, lotus flower. Nirmala treated Padma as a little sister and played with her as if she were a doll. In spite of the prayers of monks and care from traditional and Western medicine men Bina never carried another baby to full term although she conceived a number of times. Bina and Suraj were disappointed at not having a son, complained bitterly about their fate but eventually reconciled themselves to it.

Kanaka hardly ever went out but she had no lack of company. Ladies of her age respected her as the widow of a man who would have been the acknowledged leader of their community but for his untimely death. They made a point of taking turns to visit her and kept her informed of all the news that was fit to be told. She prayed for half an hour at dawn and dusk in a little prayer area she set up in the store room attached to the main room. Her prayers were those she had learned in her childhood at home and she had a simple person's faith that if she prayed regularly and lived an honest life, she would be looked after by Lord Mahavir in this life and the next. She did what she could to help Bina and Padma and did not complain when her favours were taken for granted.

There was no girls' school nearby and Nirmala's private tutoring was limited to a second grade education, basically learning to read and write Hindi. Once she learned to read there was no stopping her. She read every bit of wrapping paper that came her way. Devi was visiting when she observed Nirmala trying to read a scrap. Devi asked Nirmala, "Do you like reading?"

"Yes Buaji, I like reading. It makes me feel good," Nirmala replied.

"Will you like to read stories in a book?" Devi asked.

"That would be so wonderful. Do you have one I can read.
"I will find one for you," Devi promised.

Devi rummaged through old newspapers and magazines
Komal used to bag the purchases of his customers and found
a couple of magazines Nirmala could read. Devi became a
source of reading material from then on and Nirmala read
every word in every magazine she got even if she did not
understand much of it.

One morning Devi and Kanaka were chatting over mugs
of tea while the children were chasing each other in Devi's
small courtyard. Kanaka asked Devi how Komal's health was
after the spell of cold he had the previous week. Devi hesi-
tated a moment before replying, "Bhabhi, he has recovered
fully, thanks to Mahavirji. Something he heard in the market
he would like me to mention to you. His fellow shopkeepers
and customers think of Nirmala as the princess and Suraj as
the userpur. They feel hurt when they see Nirmala in clothes
that are a bit small for her and Padma is always in new salwar
kameez. When Nirmala is a little older she might notice the
difference and may start feeling like a poor relation of Padma
and that will not be good for her. I could help you if you will
like me to. I was always good at sewing and I have loads of
time. If you find the materials, I will do my best to have her
dressed like a princess."
    "Oh, I am so sorry. You need men to observe such things.
I want Nirmala to look and feel as good as Padma. I have
some materials in the trunk we can begin with. You tell me
when you will like some more and I will order them."

The children reacted differently to growing up in the
unusual circumstance of three closely related young families

of such disparate means living in close proximity in a tightly knit community. Padma became very arrogant, even vain. Devi's children were mild, even subservient. Thanks to her extensive reading, Nirmala developed a strong personality. With no father or a father figure to look up to and a mother who wished her well but did not know how to respond to her occasional temper tantrums, her streak of independence flowered and was to serve her well later.

Aminabad was a convenient rest stop for Shivanand on his way to and from Delhi. Once or twice a year Sarla hitched a ride with him to visit her siblings there. These visits firmed up her love for Kanaka and it bubbled over when she became a widow. Sarla had three children, all sons. Her only daughter died at birth and she grieved over her. Had she not understood how much Kanaka needed her child, she would have offered to adopt Nirmala. Instead, she welcomed Nirmala at her home several times a year.

5

Year 1931: The Western world was in the midst of economic depression which showed no signs of relenting. Mahatma Gandhi, now the spiritual as well as the political leader of India, demanded full independence and peaceful protests were staged all over the country. He led a ten day march to the ocean to protest the tax on salt. The procession attracted world wide attention. A shaken government arranged a round table conference to discuss the country's future in London. Following the traditional policy of divide and rule, the Viceroy persuaded Gandhi to exclude Muslims from his delegation and let Jinnah be their sole representative.

Shivanand had three sisters. The oldest sister, Gomti, was married to Banwari Lal, a giant of a man known for his great physical strength. He was a municipal administrator. His salary was low but the opportunities for 'income on the side' were many and he lived like a rich man. Gomti had a son and a daughter in quick succession and then another son after a ten year interval. The young Ganesh was doted on by the parents and the older siblings. He was charming and handsome, tall and athletic, the captain of his school's cricket team and the goalkeeper on the football team. His curly black hair parted in the middle enhanced his expressive face. He did not pay much attention to his studies and was by far the oldest student in high school at the age of nineteen.

It was the festival of Holi. An unusually cold winter was over and the spring mornings were pleasantly warm. Family members and friends got together to rub colourful powders on each others' faces while the younger set sprayed each other with cool coloured water. . In the later part of the morning Ganesh arrived at Shivanand's villa with his sack of powders, his wet cotton kurta and trousers, originally white now a miscellany of colours, clinging to his skin and face and hair powdered red, green and yellow. The courtyard, a hub of activity since early morning, became even more alive.

Shivanand, Sarla and visiting siblings were chatting in a corner away from the mayhem in the centre of the courtyard. Ganesh did not pay attention to splashes from the cousins and headed towards the uncles and aunts. He first touched the feet of each of them, then respectfully pasted their foreheads while answering their questions. Then he turned his attention to the younger set. He caught cousin Vijay, held him in embrace with his right hand and rubbed coloured powder on his face with his left. Vijay was wriggling without success but Ganesh had to let him go when he felt a splash of cold water on his back. He let Vijay go and turned around to face the insolent attacker. It was a young girl who was holding a bucket and giggling at his discomfort. She did not turn and try to escape, as other girls would have but stood firmly ready for his response. He looked at her sparkling mischievous eyes and petite frame and asked, "Who are you? Never seen you before."

Vijay intervened. "She is Nirmala from Aminabad, daughter of Kanaka Mausi. You know, Amma's widowed sister. I am surprised you don't remember her. She visits often. She will be with us for the summer."

"Now that he knows all about me, will someone tell me who this colourful lad is?" Nirmala demanded.

"He is Ganesh, son of Gomti Bua, Abba's sister. They live in Paltan Bazaar and he goes to Mission school. You should see him play football. Greatest goalkeeper the team ever had," Vijay responded.

Obviously pleased with the compliment, Ganesh made a suggestion, "We are playing St. Stephan from Delhi on Sunday afternoon. You should come and watch. We need supporters."

Nirmala turned towards Vijay, "Bhaiya, will you like to go to the game?"

"Yes, it will be a close game and fun to watch," Vijay replied.

"Can I come with you?" Nirmala's tone was deferential.

"Yes, if Ammaji agrees," Vijay replied.

Nirmala walked straight to Sarla, "Mausiji, Can I go with Vijay to watch a football match?"

"Where is the match? Why do you want to go? Sarla was conscious of her role as the surrogate mother.

"Ganesh is playing and Vijay says it will be fun to watch. I need some fresh air too." Nirmala made her case.

"All right so long as it is not cold or wet," Sarla granted the conditional permission.

Nirmala suppressed the scream of joy about to escape from her throat and conveyed the good news to Vijay.

On Sunday Vijay and Nirmala walked to the school playground a couple of miles away. Ganesh introduced them to the members of the team and was surprised how shy Nirmala was. But the shyness vanished when the game started. Nirmala shrieked with delight every time the ball was near the goal Ganesh was protecting. And protect he did, diving to the right or the left, jumping high to grab the corner kicks, rushing to intercept crosses. The team lifted him up at the end of the game and carried him to the sidelines where the school masters were cheering. The Headmaster said, "Good job" and patted him on the back. Vijay and Nirmala watched Ganesh with pride. "Do you always play this well," Nirmala asked when he joined them for the walk home. "No, only when there are special people watching the game," Ganesh replied. Nirmala seemed pleased and the distance home was covered much too quickly for her.

Ganesh cancelled his annual trip to visit his sister in Kismatnagar this summer. Instead, he spent his days with his cousins and their guest. In the afternoon, the boys sat in a circle on a mat on the floor of the covered verandah and played the card game Paplu and in the evenings before dinner they went for long walks under the eucalyptus trees on Chakrota Road. Paramesh was seventeen and Vijay sixteen and Nirmala only thirteen. They treated her like a child and did not include her in their games, although she was allowed to watch. One afternoon Nirmala has had enough of watching. When three had sat down to play she said with some vehemence addressing no one in particular, "Can I play too?"

Ganesh stopped shuffling and said, "Yes, that is a good idea. We can play Whist, all four of us. I am getting bored with this stupid game of Paplu."

"But she doesn't know how to play," objected Paramesh.

"I can learn," Nirmala responded.

"We can teach her. It is a simple game. She will learn quickly," Ganesh supported her.

"We can try but I don't want her as partner," Paramesh and Vijay said in unison.

"I will have her as partner and we will clobber you," Ganesh retorted.

Nirmala had a good sense of cards and before long her cousins were competing to have her as a partner. She was now asked to join them in their walks although she did not get many chances to speak. When she got tired and lagged behind, it was Ganesh who waited for her.

Summer was soon over and thundering clouds announced the arrival of the monsoons. The boys went back to school and Nirmala returned to Aminabad. She noticed that something was not quite the same; there was a constant stream of visitors and whispered conversations between her mother and uncle Suraj. Nirmala watched this for a while trying to work out what was up. Then she couldn't contain herself any longer and faced Kanaka one afternoon.

"Amma, what are you doing that you do not want me know?"

"No need to get all het up. You will be told when it is all finalized."

"If it concerns me I want to know now, not when it is final and I can do nothing about it."

"There is no point bothering your little head about it. Nothing may come out of it."

"What if something comes out that I do not like?"

"There is no way you will not like it. All right. I will tell you if you insist even though it is not settled yet. Ramesh Ji of Chilkana wants you for their son. It is a great family. Biggest zamindars in the whole district. Respected all over. The boy is known to be a good boy. No bad habits, good looking, a little short but not skinny. You will be so happy."

"I know who I am marrying. He is tall and handsome with beautiful curly hair. And he doesn't have any bad habits either."

"What are you telling me? Is this someone you know or are you imagining him?"

"I am not imagining him. I know the boy I am going to marry come what may. You can tell Ramesh Ji that Nirmala is taken. End of story."

"You are not taken till Suraj and I agree and make the match. Tell me who is the boy and I will ask Suraj to look into it."

"Don't ask Mamaji to look into it, ask him to arrange the wedding. I would rather jump in the well than marry any one else. If you don't want me to live, go ahead; arrange my wedding with Ramesh Ji or some other Ji. The day after you have done it, you can look for your only child at the bottom of the well."

The quarrel continued into the night and ended only when both were exhausted. They went to bed crying their hearts out cursing the other for ruining their lives. Their sleep was intermittent, Kanaka dreaming of life without Nirmala and the grandchildren, Nirmala dreaming of being fished out of the well by Suraj's servants. They awoke with the first rays of light. Kanaka broke the ice.

"Who is this tall handsome boy you want to waste your life on?"

"I am not wasting my life on anyone. I am so happy when I am in the same room as him even when he is talking to other boys. He will make me happier than a boy with all the goodness and the wealth you can imagine. I do not want wealth, I want Ganesh."

"Ganesh, who is this Ganesh? How do you know him?"

"He is the nephew of Shivanand Mausaji. I met him in the summer. He has won my heart."

"Oh, him. What if his family doesn't want an orphan who brought bad luck when she was born?"

"I will become a sanyasin and spend the rest of my days wandering from one holy place to the other. You won't have to worry about me."

"I don't have a good feeling about it. All the same, I will talk to Suraj and Panditji and send a letter to Sarla asking about this Ganesh. Now go back to sleep and give your eyes some rest. I don't want any one to see you with eyes red as overripe tomatoes."

Suraj was careful not to show his pleasure when Kanaka told him of Nirmala's refusal. He offered his own daughter Padma to Ramesh Ji who accepted after keeping Suraj in suspense for a while. Sarla's reply to Kanaka's enquiry was somewhat non-committal, "Ganesh's father Banwari Lal has a position with the municipality which provides ample opportunities for substantial income. He has an older brother and a sister both married. He is a handsome lad with no bad habits." Kanaka noticed the absence of any mention of job or business prospects but Nirmala's insistence left her no choice. She asked Sarla to sound out Banwari Lal and Gomti. They readily agreed to the match. A year later, eleven year old Padma's wedding had all the pomp due to a princess and fourteen year old Nirmala was married to twenty one year old Ganesh in a modest wedding appropriate for a poor cousin. Still, the dowry that accompanied Nirmala was not modest, thanks to Kanaka passing on all her jewellery and silk saris and Sarla's contribution of ten thousand rupees to the cash purse. Suraj contributed by hosting a modest reception for fifty close relatives. However, Nirmala did not notice the difference in the two weddings. She was going to spend her life with the man she loved. What more can a barely pubescent girl in her situation wish?

It is customary for a mother to shed tears when her daughter leaves for her new family. But Kanaka did not shed any. She was sending the only person in this world she could call her own into a strange world where, she felt in her bones, her groom would not be her provider and protector but a helpless baby with an adult appearance. Kanaka knew deep down that if she gave in to tears, there was no one who could stop the flood and her world would drown.

2

Early Married Years

(1932–1945)

*T*hree round table conferences held in London failed because the British were not ready to grant India independence. There were mass protests in India during the thirties and considerable communal conflict among Hindus and Muslims. Gandhi's main achievement during the period was to bring untouchables into the mainstream politics of India as Hindus. Gandhi also campaigned for the emancipation of women. In 1935 British government unilaterally proposed a federal structure for India with weak governments in the centre and the provinces who could do little without the British approval. The elections were held in 1937 and the Congress formed governments in nine of the eleven provinces. When the war started in 1939, Gandhi demanded full independence in return for support. Congress ministries resigned when the demand was turned down. All of the Congress leaders, whether Hindus, Muslims or Christians, Brahmins or untouchables, were sent to prison for the duration of war. Jinnah and his cohorts were left free to create communal trouble which led to millions of deaths over the next nine years.

Ashapur was in those days a prosperous small town in the foothills. The ground rose rapidly to the north where hill tribes scratched a meager living from terraced farms on the southern slope of the ridges. The boys of these tribes, as young as ten, were hired out to the families in the city where they worked all their waking hours for the bare minimum of food and clothing and a few rupees for the parents. Young girls were often rented out or sold outright to the businesses in the red light district. There were several small saw mills where the logs from the forests were made into posts for the construction industry. The compressed saw dust from the mills was used in small stoves for cooking and heating in many homes. The town also served as a summer resort for the less well-off members of the ruling classes. The shopkeepers supplied a large area surrounding the town and made a good living. There were tea gardens to the south and a large army base of Gurkha soldiers and British officers in the northern outskirts. The combination of relative prosperity of the townspeople, and the might of the military base, ensured that the independence movement and uprising due to communal strife, while gaining strength elsewhere in the country, did not disturb the peace in Ashapur.

Kaisthan Mohalla was a community of families in comfortable circumstances in the old part of town. Most of the residents were small shopkeepers with a sprinkling of tradesmen and Brahmins. The streets were wide; a horse cart could pass a bullock cart without much manipulation. The homes were built around a courtyard where women congregated for gossip. Children played on the street without the danger of being run over because cars were rare and carts accommodating. Homes were built with bricks and plaster; the walls were white-washed inside and out. Banwari Lal lived in the largest home on the street. The ground floor of the house had the kitchen and storage on one side of the enclosed courtyard, a lavatory and a bathroom on the opposite side and two large rooms on the other side facing the entrance. The rooms had marble tile floors of alternating black and white squares and large windows opening to the street. The windows had vertical wrought iron bars to keep thieves out. The courtyard and utility rooms had concrete floors as did the kitchen. It was about eight feet by eight feet, there were alcoves on one side for pots and pans and a slightly raised platform for cooking with a couple of sawdust stoves placed against the wall. On special occasions when several dishes were to be cooked, a corner of the courtyard became the extra kitchen with one or more stoves. Family members sat around the cook in the kitchen, each on a patra, a wooden stool about three inches high, with a brass plate on the floor in front of them. Hot chapattis were served straight from tawa, a slightly concave sauce pan without a handle. Chapatis were eaten with one or two vegetable and lentil curries and some yogurt in small brass bowls around the chapatti on the plate. Next to each plate was a tumbler with cool water from a large earthen pitcher. Fingers of the right hand served as knives and forks. It was not good form to touch food with left hand.

The bathroom was small with no taps or wash basin so a bucket with water was placed on the floor. The water was cold in the summer and warm in the winter. A bather sat on a patra and used a small jug to pour water from the bucket over his body. The lavatory was the smallest room in the house. It had no flush. There was a raised platform with a well placed hole. A bucket under the hole collected the waste matter. Jamadar, the lavatory man, collected the buckets from the neighbourhood in the midmorning and deposited the contents in a municipal facility. He or she also washed the floor with water and detergent—it would not be appropriate for someone of the upper classes to have anything do with the lavatory other than use it. There was no toilet paper; a wet left hand did the job.

There were three rooms upstairs: another lavatory, a bathroom and an open area to enjoy the cool breeze in summer evenings and the morning sun in the winter. It had been a good house to bring up their three children. Ganesh was the youngest by ten years. The older brother Yagni and the sister Parvati now lived with their own families in Kismatnagar three hundred miles away. The thought of her baby moving away and leaving her in the big house by herself disturbed Gomti. She suggested to her husband that they should move upstairs and let Ganesh and Nirmala occupy the ground floor and run the household as one family of four. Banwari Lal agreed for a very practical reason; he knew that Ganesh was not yet ready to strike out on his own.

Ganesh was a sportsman and had no inclination for studies. He had repeatedly failed his High School finals and Banwari Lal decided that owning a small business was his son's future. What could be better than owning a garage to repair the vehicle of the future, the motor car? Thanks to the poor state of roads, cars needed repairs often and Shameer, his nephew, couldn't handle all the work coming into his garage. Banwari Lal persuaded him to train Ganesh in all aspects of the business from changing oil to repairing gear shaft, from hiring workers to keeping books. Working for money was something new and Ganesh was nervous about it and still hesitating when Nirmala joined the family six months after the wedding. She pointed out that his parents could not support them for ever and he had to make a living somehow. Owning the garage was as good as anything and worth a try.

She sent a servant to call the barber to cut his hair, gave the maid his shirt and English pants to iron and leather shoes to shine. On the following Monday, she made sure he had bathed and dressed for work in good time and then served him the breakfast of jalebis and hot milk. He did not see her waving to him as he passed the window on his way to the garage.

This was a traditional family and Nirmala was expected to cover her face when in the presence of any older man whether related or not. One afternoon a few days after her arrival, Nirmala was sitting on the mat reading a story by Munshi Premchand when her father-in-law walked by. Nirmala quickly covered her head but not the face. Banwari Lal awkwardly looked the other way and went into the nearest room. He pointed out the lack of decorum in his daughter-in-law to his wife. Gomti, keen to establish her authority in the family hierarchy, came out with her eyes blazing.

"What do you mean by this?"

"Mataji, why are you so angry?"

"Don't be insolent. Asking me why I am angry? I am angry because your Babaji is embarrassed. Do you need me to tell you why?"

"Yes Mataji. I said and did nothing except cover my head. Should I have got up to touch his feet?"

"How stupid of me I let that Sarla persuade me to accept a village idiot in the family. I should have known what I was getting into."

"Mataji, please don't be so upset. It couldn't be that bad. I did not say or do anything."

"It is what you did not do that is upsetting. You know you are not to show your face to your Babaji. Or to any other older male relative. Did not your mother tell you? Do I have to teach you how to behave?"

"Mataji, Amma did tell me. But I do not know what have I done that I need to hide my face? Or there is something repulsive in my appearance. You must tell me so I know what is wrong."

"There is nothing wrong with your face or your appearance. But a bride does not show her face to men in her husband's family. It has always been thus and it will always be thus. Do you understand?"

"Mataji, I am sorry I do not understand. It may have always been thus but it will be different from now on. You know I respect Babaji more than any man, not having known my father. I will show respect by covering my head but I will not cover my face. I want to see where I am going and I want every one to see what I am thinking rather than hide my feelings behind a curtain."

"Bas, bas, enough of the lip. I will discuss the issue with Ganesh and he will tell you how to behave. Go down now and stay out of my sight till you have learned elementary manners."

Nirmala walked down slowly, tears streaming down her cheeks. Her sari slipped off her head but she didn't care.

Ganesh came home in the evening more irritable than tired. It was his fourth day in the garage, yet another day spent doing jobs he thought were beneath him. Gomti called Ganesh as soon as she heard his footsteps, "Ganesh, come upstairs, I have some urgent matter to discuss with you."

"Can it wait till I washed my hands and face?"

"I have been waiting for you for the whole afternoon. Come up straight away."

Gomti was sitting cross-legged on a divan with the window behind her. His sooty face and greasy hands revolted her. She felt sorry for her baby who had to do the dirty work to support that village bumpkin and her anger at Nirmala's response mounted further. She screamed at the top of her voice, "Do you want to know what that girl did today? Can the Princess of Aminabad do whatever she feels like doing, even if her deeds destroy the good name of this family?" People walking on the street sensed that an interesting drama was unfolding and cupped their hands over the ears to make sure they didn't miss anything.

"Mataji, tell me all about it. I will make sure it doesn't happen again."

Gomti described the incident with some ornamentation and followed it by a long spiel on how her daughter-in-law was expected to behave in her respectable household. Ganesh listened attentively but did not know what to do. He was very tense when he came downstairs. However, a look at his bride's swollen face was enough to evaporate any idea of a lecture on family tradition. He sat down by her side and asked what had happened. Nirmala told her side of the story with the final statement, "I am proud of who I am. I have nothing to hide from. I am not going around with my face covered whatever the custom." The stream of tears continued to flow.

"Let me think about it. We have to find a solution somehow," Ganesh said in a consoling tone. For the next few days the two generations avoided each other till the issue was unexpectedly resolved.

It was Banwari Lal's custom to drop by at the end of the week and have a scotch with Shivanand. After the usual pleasantries on the next visit, he mentioned the incident and asked for advice. Shivanand's reply surprised him, "It is a silly custom of a backward country. I never saw a woman covering her face in England. It is brave of that girl to fight for progress and you should support her." Later that day when they were having their usual drink of scotch on the rocks, Banwari Lal told Gomti of his conversation with her brother and peace returned to the household.

2

A few months had gone by when Shameer visited Banwari Lal in his office. After mandatory Chai, he asked the attendant to close the door. He faced his uncle but did not look at him. His voice was very soft when he spoke "Chachaji, I am sorry to have to tell you what I see in my garage and you can tell me what I should do."

"What have you seen?"

"I have noticed that Ganesh does not like to get his hands dirty and is not interested in learning the work. I have tried him in different jobs; the result is always the same. He wastes his time and that of the others. All he can do is talk about the great performances when he was the hero of his school team."

"Why do you think Ganesh does this?"

"It appears as if he is afraid that what he does will not be good enough and covers it up by bragging about his past to other workers. This complex shows up again when I introduce him to a client. He clams up and creates a bad impression."

"What is your conclusion?"

"I am afraid he is not meant for this job. He has a lot of growing up to do before he can handle a business. I will be happy for you to visit the garage yourself and check the situation out. I agree that he needs to find something that he can do. Unfortunately, it doesn't seem to be in my garage."

"Well, Shameer, it is good of you to bring me into the picture. I do not need to check it out. I will talk to Ganesh tonight. You do not need to pay him for the work he did not do. From what you just said you will not miss him if today is his last day with you."

"Thank you Chachaji, for being so understanding. This is best for all of us. Please be kind and let me know when I can be of service to you."

After dinner Banwari Lal asked Ganesh to join him in his room.

"Close the door and sit down," he said pointing to a chair and heading for the divan. Something in his demeanour made Ganesh nervous and he did as he was told. Then he heard his father say gently, "Shameer came over to see me today. He doesn't want you in his garage. He thinks that you don't like to get your hands dirty and are not suited to work in his place. What do you have to say?"

"Babaji, the work is very hard. It is all physical work, just like a labourer. You would be ashamed of me if you saw me doing what Shameer wants me to do."

"The idea was for you to learn the operation of a garage by working there. You can't tell someone what to do unless you know how to do it. You don't want to work like a labourer. I understand that. But what do you want to work as?"

"I want to have a shop, any shop. I buy things cheap at wholesale and sell them at a profit to the public. Give me some time to find out what kind of shop will be the best and how much money it will need to set up."

"OK, I will wait for you. But not too long. Remember that I do not have much to leave to you and so you have to find the means to look after your family."

Ganesh left the room his eyes glued to the floor. He had postponed the day of reckoning. As to the warning of Babaji, it was not in his nature to worry, least of all about practical things like earning a living.

Another few months passed. Ganesh whiled away the days visiting his former school buddies, drinking endless cups of tea, gossiping about their acquaintances and playing cards. Most of these young men were in similar situation. They had no particular skills for jobs where they could earn a reasonable living and believed that working in low-paid unskilled jobs was bad for the reputation of their families. They did not face the unpleasant fact that you need either capital or hard work—often both—to succeed and dreamed of businesses which produced big profits with small capital and little work. Of course they did not find such business. They lived with their parents and did not feel pressured about their financial needs. They could always persuade their mothers to part with small sums for pocket money. Ganesh had access to cash from the dowry deposited with Shivanand because Shivanand did not fuss with small withdrawals.

One evening Ganesh returned home to be greeted by Nirmala who had thrown up every thing she ate that day. She did not know why and was too scared of her mother-in-law to tell her. Ganesh did not know what it was either. He went upstairs to Gomti to confirm that a doctor was needed. Gomti's reaction was completely unexpected, "Why didn't Nirmala tell me herself? Why does my family keep all the good news from me?"

"What is good about vomitting, Mataji? She is looking so pale and sick."

"Aray Bhaiya, don't the young of this generation know anything any more? She does not need a doctor, she needs a midwife. Send someone to Daiji and attend to your wife. Make her comfortable and attend to her needs. I need a grandson to play with. Those in Kismatnagar are no good to me."

Ganesh was delighted at the turn of events. He sent Manohar, a servant, to fetch Daiji who had helped bring him, his siblings and some of the nephews and nieces into the world. Nirmala looked up after vomitting in a basin and saw the beaming face of Ganesh. She was furious, "Why are you so happy when I am so sick, What did Mataji give you?"

"I am happy because you are going to be a mother. Mataji says this sickness will pass in a day or two. Mohan has gone to fetch Daiji. She should be here soon," Ganesh explained.

"Oh, I want to be a mother. But I hope it does not hurt too much. I have heard of mothers dying in childbirth. I don't want to die. I want to live and look after my children, girls and boys," Nirmala said as Ganesh led her towards the string bed.

"You will be all right. We will have Dr. Mitra check on you and he will be by your bedside if there is even the smallest problem. I want children, but I want you more than them, much more." Ganesh was utterly honest when he said this.

Ganesh helped her lie comfortably in bed, covered her with a cotton sheet and indulged in the usual talk of a new expectant father. Nirmala lay in bed silently, smiling faintly every time she looked at her husband's excited face. She had just closed her eyes when Daiji came bustling in. She sent Ganesh out, felt around Nirmala's stomach, confirmed the verdict of Gomti and assured the family that all was well. But Daiji did not make any further contribution to the pregnancy. As was the convention, despite the protests of Ganesh, Nirmala returned to Aminabad three months before the baby was due. Kanaka, Bina and Devi had begun preparations for the birth when they heard the news of the expected arrival of first child in the second generation. Devi sewed the clothes for the baby, Bina ordered a cot to be made and Kanaka knitted little blankets and sweaters. Nirmala received a warm welcome when she arrived by bus accompanied by Ganesh. After settling Nirmala, Kanaka took Ganesh to a different room and asked searching questions about his career plans. His vague answers and general discomfort confirmed her previous doubts. Ganesh sensed her hostility and left for Ashapur after two days instead of staying a week or two as he had planned.

———◇◇———

Nirmala mostly rested and walked over short distances as the baby grew inside her. She felt the baby kicking and wished Ganesh was there to share her joy. But Ganesh did not want to face Kanaka before he had some good news for her and stayed away. It was a happy time for Nirmala in other ways. A week after the due date, a bouncy boy was delivered by the midwife to everyone's delight. He was named Santosh, contentment in Hindi. One month after the birth Nirmala and Santosh returned to Ashapur in Shivanand's car to a great welcome by the extended family.

Ganesh had still not decided on the business he wanted to start. Nirmala was too busy with the baby to worry about Ganesh's inability to earn a living and too young to be concerned with considerations such as where the money to meet their daily needs would come from. Even if someone warned her that the dowry she brought with her was being depleted, she would not have cared. Ganesh was loving and considerate, paid attention to her smallest wish and defended her from the attacks of his mother. Never an unkind word slipped out of his mouth. Their lovemaking was more delightful than she had ever dreamed of. Now that she had an adorable baby, her cup of happiness was full.

To keep Babaji off his back Ganesh became a partner in a store owned by a couple of retirees from Gurkha regiment that sold electric supplies and hired electricians to wire new and old homes. It was a great time to be in this business because older areas of the city and the surrounding villages were being connected to a power grid and needed electricians to wire the homes and hook them up with the grid. However, he knew little about wiring and was not interested in merchandising. He considered the store a place away from home where his friends could visit and shoot the breeze over

chai and samosas from the stall next door. The other owners did not mind because they had a sucker for a partner
who was easily persuaded to put more money in the business
without asking why it was needed or where the proceeds of
the sales were going. Ganesh did occasionally worry that the
dowry pot was shrinking but it was not something he worried Nirmala with. She had a lot on her plate with a new baby
arriving every fifteen months. Satya was next. The third baby
died of cholera soon after he was two. Ravi, the fourth, survived serious bouts of illness in his first year. A baby girl was
next but she was not as fortunate and succumbed to pneumonia before she was three months old. Two months before
she was twenty three Nirmala gave birth to her sixth child on
a cold December evening. A week later she was hard at work
looking after four boys aged six and younger. Nirmala did not
expect Ganesh to be different than other men. She was glad
to see him play with the children in the evenings but the idea
of sharing the work load never crossed their minds.

3

Year 1942: The war in Europe spread to Africa and Northeast
Asia. Gandhi and other Congress leaders demanded independence before agreeing to support the British and were
jailed for the duration of the war. The Muslim League offered
verbal support and their leader, Jinnah, was busy strength-
ening his party's presence among the Muslims and spread-
ing hatred for Hindus among them. Once again heavy taxes
were imposed and the Indian treasury was drained to support Britain in the war. There was a famine in Bengal and
several million men, women and children starved to death
while the government shipped grain to the British army on
the eastern warfront.

It was a harsh winter and nights had been bitterly cold. A month after the birth of Nirmala's sixth child, Gomti opened her eyes one morning earlier than usual. The cold sunlight filtered into the room through the gaps in the closed window. As Gomti pulled her quilt over her head she heard what sounded like moans from her husband's bed across the room.

"Are you all right?" she asked with some irritation.

"I do not feel well. I feel hot."

Gomti was alarmed. She went to his bed and touched his forehead. "You have a fever. Do you have a headache as well?"

He opened his eyes with some effort and looked at his wife's worried face, "Yes, but it is not bad. Nothing that a cup of tea won't fix."

"You don't ever listen to me. I told you to see Dr. Mitra when you started sniffling a month ago. But you have to try Ayurvedic powders first. It is the same every time. Try the powders till you can't get out of bed. Then call the proper doctor. I am sending for Dr. Mitra. Don't worry; I will bring you the tea as well. Not that it will reduce the fever."

Dr. Mitra had studied medicine in England and had served as the army doctor for a number of years. He had married a nurse from the London hospitalat which he trained and their lifestyle was that of an English couple living in the colonies. He liked the routine of a leisurely breakfast of fried bacon and eggs with lightly buttered toast and was irritated when when the butler interrupted with, "Sir, the servant of Banwari Ji is here. His master is very sick and you are needed as soon as you can get there."

"Tell him I will be there in an hour." The good doctor finished his coffee, put on a woolen suit and his winter coat and checked his medical bag before giving it to the servant to carry it to the vintage Morris Minor.

The toot of the car horn announced Dr. Mitra's arrival and Gomti met him at the door. He examined his patient thoroughly under the watchful eyes of the anxious family. Examination finished, he stood up straight. The family was relieved to see his countenance relax, even more when he pronounced, "He caught some infection at work There is nothing much of concern." He handed the prescription for a syrup to Ganesh, "My pharmacist can mix this from local ingredients. It should reduce his fever." He turned to Nirmala, "How is the baby doing."

"Doctor Sahib, do you have some time to see the baby and me too?"

"Yes of course. Better now than later." She led him downstairs to the baby. One look at the baby was enough to worry the good doctor. He picked the baby up to estimate his weight and then examined him thoroughly. He turned to Nirmala and asked, "Are you feeding him or is he on the bottle?"

"I am feeding him but I don't think I have enough milk for him. He cries a lot as if he is hungry, sucks lustily but he doesn't get much. Do you think I should put him on the bottle?"

"The formula for baby bottles is hard to get these days. The war has stopped most imports and the local stuff is adulterated with who knows what. Can you get a wet nurse? You may find a pahari woman if you ask around."

"I have several friends from Almora who can find the right woman for us. I will ask them," Ganesh replied.

"Please treat this matter as urgent. The baby is not growing at all. He needs much more than he is getting and as soon as possible," Dr. Mitra said.

As he turned to leave Nirmala piped up "Doctor sahib, I have one more problem. Do you have time to examine me too?'

"Yes, of course," Dr. Mitra replied and then turned to Ganesh, "You go out while I check Nirmala's problem."

———◇◇———

Dr. Mitra found Nirmala in good health and complimented her on a fine recovery. "So what is the problem?" he asked.

"Doctor Sahib," Nirmala said, "six babies in seven years are enough. I do not want to go through this cycle again. Is there something you can give me to stop having more children?"

"The easiest way is to keep Ganesh out of your bed," Dr. Mitra said with a smile.

"I can't. He won't stay out and I am not sure I want to keep him out. Is there no other way?"

"The only thing I can do is to take the womb out. It is not a dangerous operation. But you will need to rest for at least a month after it."

"What will taking the womb out do to the rest of my body? Will he be put off me after the operation?"

"It doesn't make any difference to the rest of your body. As for Ganesh, he will not notice any difference, I can assure you."

"Thank you Doctor Sahib, you have taken a huge load off me. I will have the operation as soon as you can do it. I will write to Amma. I am sure she will pay for it if it is not too much and she will be happy to be with me when I am recovering. The children love her so much, they won't miss me."

"It is not much—less than a hundred rupees. Ask her to come next week. Keep Ganesh out of your bed till then."

"Thank you Doctor Sahib, thank you from the bottom of my heart."

No sooner had Dr. Mitra left then Gomti rushed into the room and demanded, "What were you discussing so secretly with Doctor Sahib? What is wrong with you?"

"Mataji, nothing is wrong. He checked me and said every thing is good. I asked him what I could do to not have any more children."

"Why don't you want more children? My other son has given me four grandsons and two granddaughters; my daughter has given me eight granddaughters and two grandsons. Why should I be content with only four from the son who lives with me?"

"Mataji, I am exhausted with carrying and delivering babies. If I have any more I will fall ill. Then who will look after them. I have to stop for their sake."

"Ha, have to stop for their sake! I told Babaji we were bringing a weakling into the family. But no one listens to me. Why did you not ask me first? Have you asked Ganesh? He should have some say in it too. Or my son doesn't matter?"

"I have not asked him. But he loves me and he wants me to live a long life. I know I will not live long if I become pregnant again."

"How can you not become pregnant? Are you going to keep my son out of your bed and make him go to the prostitutes?"

"Mataji, Doctor Sahib said he can do an operation next week. He will take the womb out and after a month I will be as good as ever. And your son will not notice any difference."

"Who will look after you and the children when you are in bed? You know I am fully occupied with your Babaji."

"I will ask Amma to come over. She loves to be with the children and she will be happy to look after every one. She gets lonely in Aminabad and this will do her some good too."

"I don't have a good feeling about it. I wanted so much to have a granddaughter to play with. Oh Bhagwan! The world has changed. Our children make decisions without asking us. If we did that in my day we would be thrown out of the house on our behinds."

"Mataji, you are more understanding and loving than most parents. I am so fortunate to have such a compassionate mother-in-law."

The praise softened Gomti. She patted Nirmala's shoulder before saying, "Leave flattery alone. You talk to Ganesh about this operation and I will get the blessing of Babaji. Things go better when you have the blessings of elders in the family"

When Nirmala told Ganesh of her decision that evening his reaction did not surprise her in the least, "Hooray, we can have fun all year with no worries."
"You read my mind" Nirmala responded.

Ganesh hated the idea of parting with the baby who Gomti said looked exactly like him. Moreover, he felt that the last baby should be the one to be cherished the most. However, he could not come up with an alternative solution and found a wet nurse in Chakrota, one day away on foot. She collected Rishi, put him to her breast and the hungry infant fed greedily. She thankfully accepted parathas and subzi for her trip back home, wrapped the baby in a shawl and lodged him in a loop in her sari on the back and set off. Two years to the day, she returned with a healthy toddler who had been forgotten by every one but Ganesh and Nirmala.

4

Dr. Mitra saved Nirmala from any more children but he could not help Babaji. What he thought was an ordinary cold soon became pneumonia. After examing his old friend he became grave and said to Ganesh, "The infection is not serious and it is easily curable with imported drugs. However, we have a major problem. Thanks to the war in Europe, civil disobedience all over India and the clamp down on imports by the Raj, the country has run out of medicines. I will prescribe you three. Get whichever one is available. Come and see me if you can't get any." Ganesh went from pharmacy to pharmacy, tried different prescriptions, got a letter from Shivanand asking pharmacists to fill the prescription as a special favour to him, but with no luck. They tried traditional medicines in desperation but Babaji got steadily worse. He hung on for a couple of months till one spring afternoon, when he opened his eyes and whispered, "Hare Ram, Hare Krishna, Jai Mahavir." His grip on Gomti's hand loosened and then his hand slipped on to bed. Gomti let out a scream, "Hai Bhagwan" and began sobbing and pulling her grey hair which had not been washed for months.

Babaji's death took away the hand that guided the family. Worse, the financial backbone was no more. Babaji's pension for the widow was small and the extra under-the-table payments ended as soon as the illegal services stopped. It hit Gomti particularly hard. She took to drink, Ballentine's Scotch, nothing but the best. In her addled mind she blamed Nirmala for her misfortunes. On rare occasions she was not in drunken stupor she supported herself on the railing overlooking the courtyard and shouted curses on Nirmala. "I never wanted you as my daughter-in-law, you brought death to your father and grandfather, misery to your mother and now on us. I knew it all along but Sarla forced you on me. Hai Bhagwan, what sins did I commit in my past life to be encumbered with such a Bahu." Nirmala kept the children away when she could and wept bitterly when Ganesh came home. Poor Ganesh! There was nothing he could do to stop Mataji; they had to bear the burden of her grief as well as their own.

One evening Ganesh came home earlier than usual looking very glum. He barely touched his dinner and did not even look at the Kheer with raisins and cashew nuts, his favourite dish. Nirmala's worries now shifted focus from her mother-in-law and children to her husband. She asked gently, "What is upsetting you. Did something happen at the shop?"

"Yes, and it looks bad. The importer in Delhi wants ten thousand rupees before he will send us any supplies. The shelves are empty. I need two thousand rupees for my share."

"Why don't you get it out of our account? I brought twenty five thousand rupees in dowry."

"There is nothing left from that money." Nirmala was shocked. "How come you spent all my money and never told me about it?"

"I took small amounts out when we needed it and did not want to bother you with it. I was surprised myself when Munimji told me it was all gone."

"What are we going to do now?"

Ganesh answered sheepishly "I was thinking that if you could let me have your necklace, I could get the money from Mahajan, the userer. That will keep the shop going."

Nirmala's face turned red, "What happens if I don't give you the necklace. Amma will never forgive me if she finds out. It is one memory she has of Babuji."

After a pause Ganesh blurted, "We will lose the shop. All the money and my work of the last three years will be for nothing."

Nirmala's fury now exceeded the devotion of a wife for her husband. "I never trusted those Pahari friends of yours. Tell them to go back to their homes in the hills. It is no good throwing good money after bad. If I sell my jewelry it will be to feed my children, not for the drinks of your worthless chums."

Ganesh did not expect such a firm refusal from Nirmala. But he was not ready to give up; there was too much at stake. After Nirmala had gone to sleep, he crept upstairs. He repeated the sad tale to his mother who was, as usual, in a drunken stupor. "How many rupees did you say you need?" she asked in a blurry voice.

"Only two thousand, Mataji."

"Only two thousand? How many months pension is this two thousand?"

"Mataji, you don't look at it in terms of pension. Look at it in terms of money in your safe. You can not think of a better use of this money than to save your son's honour."

"How many bottles of whisky is this two thousand rupees?"

"Mataji, think of my shop, not of your whisky. You can manage without a drink for a while for the sake of your son, can't you?"

"Oh dear. It is hard enough to manage without your father. No, I can not do without the drink."

"Mataji, if you do not help me how will I show my face to anyone?"

" Leave me alone. I need a drink before my sleep. Pass the bottle on your way out, the glass is almost empty."

5

Although Shivanand was not known for his generosity to his relations, Ganesh had nothing to lose in asking for help. But he had to do it carefully. First he had to decide whether to see him at home or in his office. The office was on the ground floor of the palatial home. It had own entrance from the main road between the municipal administration building and the mosque. It consisted of a modest oblong room with a desk and a chair along the shorter wall where Shivanand attended to his work. Munimji, the accountant, sat cross-legged on the floor behind a low desk with the ledger and faced the door. Visitors entered the room quietly and respectfully and waited for the nod from Shivanand. There was no privacy from Munimji or other visitors. Ganesh did not like the prospect of being chastised in the office. It would be best, he decided, to catch his uncle while he was at home, before he left for work. There was always the possibility that he would be in a better mood after a good breakfast. Shivanand usually ate alone in a large dining room which seated fifty guests for dinner on celebratory occasions and was decorated to entertain the Viceroy. The breakfast was served at 8:30 sharp and consisted of porridge followed by two fried eggs, three slices of bacon and two slices of buttered toast, a habit Shavanand had acquired during his student days in England. He read the Hindustan Times for fifteen minutes while sipping tea. When the clock chimed for 9:00 o'clock he got up, took his cane from Ramlal, the butler, and limped down to his office.

Ganesh and Nirmala were born to parents who belonged to the offshoot of Hinduism called Jain whose members follow the teachings of Holy Massenger Mahavir. Nirmala prayed in a Jain temple every Tuesday morning but Ganesh prayed only when he was in trouble. His idol was Hanuman, known as the Monkey God. Hanuman plays a major role in Hindu epic Ramayan, story of the battle between the Lord Ram and the Devil Ravan, To humiliate Ram, Ravan kidnapped his wife Sita and took her to his realm in Sri Lanka. Hanuman, leader of an extinct tribe who are supposed to have looked like monkeys, acquired a godlike status among his followers by helping Ram in the war to recover Sita. A Hanuman temple was on his way to Shivanand's mansion and Ganesh stopped there to make an offering of rice and sugar candy. He arrived at the dining room five minutes before nine. Ramlal greeted him, "Ganeshji, what brings you here this morning?"

Ganesh slipped a rupee to Ramlal, "It is an urgent matter. What sort of mood is Mamaji in?"

"I noticed nothing unusual. He seems to have enjoyed his eggs and bacon," Ramlal replied.

Ganesh stood just inside the door and waited for Shivanand to notice him. Minutes passed and his patience ran out. He said barely loud enough for his partially deaf uncle to hear, "Mamaji, namaste."

Shivanand put the cup down with a clatter, "Ganesh, good to see you. How is Gomti Bibi, how is the rest of the family?"

"Your kindness sir, everyone is in good health. Nirmala asked me to convey her regards."

"Sit down, have a cup of tea. But I have to leave in a minute." He asked the butler to pour.

"Mamaji, I have a special request," Ganesh said and then added, "I wouldn't have disturbed you for something ordinary."

"What do you need? Surely Gomti and Nirmala are looking after you."

"Yes indeed sir. They do look after me very well. But you are the only person who can help me with what I have to ask."

"You make me feel more important than I deserve to be. What can I do for you?"

"Mamaji, you are in a hurry. I will make my story short. Our shop has run out of goods. The supplier in Delhi will not ship them unless we pay in advance. He says what with the war and Congress protests these are difficult times, he must have his money first."

"How much money do you need?"

"Mamaji, only two thousand rupees."

Shivanand raised his voice, "Only two thousand rupees! Why do you come to me for money? What happened to all the cash you got at your wedding, all the money Banwari left? Don't tell me you have burnt it all."

"Mamaji, don't be angry. The money was spent on the needs of the family. If there was some left I would not have troubled you."

"You have spent what was to be the capital on daily needs. Now you come to me to lend you some more. What kind of fool you take your Mamaji for. You expect him to throw his good money on your bad business. I won't do it." He drained the cup and said, "Ramlal, pass the cane."

———◇◇———

Ramlal handed Shivanand the cane and pulled the chair back. Shivanand left the dining room without another word to Ganesh who stood sheepishly next to his chair. Ramlal brought a tray and cleared the table. He had witnessed many such scenes before and knew that silence was his best option.

Ganesh left the mansion downhearted even though what happened was what he had anticipated. Only one possibility was left: Mahajan, a moneylender who lent money at exorbitant interest, but this too was only a distant hope; no userer would lend such large sums without security. But Ganesh had to give him a try. It was only a small detour to his shop and Ganesh found him sitting on a cushion on the floor leaning back on a round pillow and talking animatedly to his assistant. When he heard the footsteps he looked up, "Ganesh Ji, haven't seen you for a long time. How have you been? How is Mataji? How is Bhabhiji? What brings you to my humble abode?"

"Mahajan maharaj, everyone is well. I am here to give you a small trouble," and Ganesh explained his need in great detail.

"Two thousand rupees, that is all. It can be arranged. The house is not in your name. Did you bring some gold to leave with me?"

"Maharaj, the gold that was promised with Nirmala is still in her mother's safe in Aminabad," Ganesh lied and added, "You have known our family for a long time. Surely our word is good enough. I am not going to disappear for a mere two thousand rupees."

"It is not two thousand rupees I worry about. It is our relationship. These are difficult times. If something unpleasant happens to the shop you will have so many problems you will forget about Maharaj and his rupees. Whatever I do then will be a strain on the good relations our families have always had. No Ganesh, I will not do it. It will be bad for both of us."

Ganesh expected this response but still his disappointment was acute. His shop was gone, he had failed as a businessman and he had no skills for a job. He walked home with his head bowed and tears on his cheeks. The images of his wife, mother, uncle and the moneylender refusing to help him ran in his head like the film which repeated itself endlessly. He had one piece of good fortune; he was saved the embarrassment of runnig into a friend.

Nirmala was sewing a button on a shirt when Ganesh came in. She looked at her husband's despondent face, felt sorry for him and although she knew what was troubling him asked softly, "What is the matter? Are you all right?" But Ganesh did not look at her, let alone answer. He went to his bed on the other side of the room and lay down facing the wall. Nirmala finished sewing, went to him and sat down on the bed. She put her right hand on his shoulder and sat still for a while waiting for a response. When there was none she spoke kindly, her hand still on his shoulder. "There is nothing to be unhappy about. The shop was a sinkhole for all our money. We got nothing out of it and are better rid of it."

Ganesh turned around. His eyes were red. "Now that I lost my shop I have nothing to call mine. I have nowhere to go to. There are no jobs that I can do. I can not become a labourer. I have no skills. How will we live?"

"We need to think about what we should do. With Mataji's daily taunts we can't do it living here. We should go away for a while where we could have some peace of mind. We can go to Haridwar for summer when children do not have school. If we bathe in the holy Ganges and pray, Bhagwan will show us the path we should follow."

"Let me think about it. I will ask Mataji whether she will loan me five hundred rupees. We have to eat."

"Don't ask Mataji. Kiran is always eyeing my red sari. I will ask her what she will pay for it. All that gold thread should be worth something."

Nirmala went back to mend the children's clothes. Ganesh fell asleep. Of course he had no other idea.

Soon after he heard movement upstairs the following afternoon, Ganesh took to Gomti a glass of strong chai and six gulab jamuns he had bought from a sweet shop. She seemed pleased with the offering but was suspicious all the same. "These are good gulam jamuns," she said as an introduction before rubbing salt in the wound, "How will you spend your days now that you don't have a shop to go to?"

"Mataji, if it agrees with you, we will like to take a pilgrimage to Haridwar for a month or two," Ganesh replied controlling his anger.

"You want me to be alone, do you? Old women need looking after. What will happen to me if I fall ill?

"Mataji, I will find a maid to stay with you when we are away. What little she will charge would be worth the peace you will have without the children."

"All right. Send me a note with your address after you get there."

Nirmala shed a tear while packing her favourite sari and a short note in a cloth bag. She called Santosh who was playing on the street with neighbourhood kids, "Take this to Kiran Mausi and come back straight away. Be careful and don't drop it. Let me know when you are back," she said giving him the bag.

Kiran was not flush with cash but what she paid must have been enough. Ganesh and Nirmala packed the minimum they would need in two metal trunks and took a three hour bus ride to Haridwar two weeks later.

6

After descending from heaven on to the Gangotri glacier in the Himalayas, sacred waters cascade for a hundred miles before arriving in Haridwar and continuing their one thousand mile journey across the plains to the Bay of Bengal. A bath in the river Ganges at sunrise accompanied by the chanting of appropriate mantras washes the sins of devout Hindus away. Haridwar, the holiest of the chain of holy cities along the Ganges, is situated at the foot of the mountain range where the river flows languidly in a channel almost half a kilometer wide. Aptly named Gate to God, pilgrims come here from all over the country, some by train, others on buses and a few on foot. There are several ghats, bathing areas, each named after a particular deity with a small temple where devotees pray after their dip in the holy river. Each Ghat also has a dharmshala, where pilgrims stay in small rooms built around a courtyard. Toilet facilities are shared; washing and cooking are done in the courtyard. Payment is voluntary and most pilgrims stay for free.

Ganesh, Nirmala and their children made their way to dharmshala in Hanuman Ghat where they were given two small rooms for six of them. This was to be their home till Ganesh got instructions from above on how to make a living.

But no amount of baths in holy Ganges, prayers and offerings of rice and sweets in the temple was enough to melt the divine heart of stone. Two months passed yet Ganesh did not receive any directions. However, he did get a telegram from Ashapur. His mother was dying and she wanted him by her bedside. They packed their trunks and returned home the next morning.

Ganesh ran from the horse cart straight to his mother's room upstairs. The shriveled form of his mother lay in bed. His brother Yagni and sister Parvati had already arrived from Kismatnagar and were sitting on wooden chairs by the bedside. Parvati led Ganesh out of the room and whispered, "Mataji had a stroke soon after you left and has not opened her eyes since. She is not long for this world, you are lucky she has survived this long." Nirmala heard these words as she came upstairs and, forgetting all past humiliations, burst into tears.

Gomti passed away that night.

3

Wayward Son

(1938–1961)

෧෨෯෧෨෯෧

*T*he world war raged from 1939 to 1945. The war caused enormous destruction and exhausted both sides. Churchill won the war for Britain but lost the election which followed. The victorious Labour Party wanted to get out of India as soon as it could be done. The British government gave in to the demands of Muhammed Ali Jinnah and on August 15, 1947 two countries, Islamic Republic of Pakistan and the secular state of India were born. Massive rioting broke out resulting in almost a million dead and fourteen million displaced.

1

We go back seven years before the death of Gomti and before the birth of last two children of Nirmala We are still in Ashapur at the home of Banwari Lal with Gomti, Ganesh and Nirmala. The year is 1938, the month is September. It is a pleasant time of the year. The heat of summer is long gone, monsoon season is over and the harshness of winter is a couple of months away.

Pandit Hari Ram had promised to bring the horoscope at ten. The whole family and some neighbours gathered on a mat in the courtyard with Nirmala sitting in the middle. She held her new baby, their fourth son, in her arms. The baby had recently been fed and was sound asleep. A long black mark on his forehead protected him from an evil eye. Ganesh, aided by their servant Manohar, a fourteen year old short skinny boy from the hillside, was making sure that every one had the drink they wanted, tea or nimbu pani—cold water with lemon and sugar. Neighbours were complimenting the beauty and health of the baby boy. Three older brothers and the children of visiting relatives were merrily running around upstairs on the balcony which overlooked the courtyard. Panditji, an old man almost bent double with age, was wearing a saffron loin cloth and vest, his forehead covered in white ash when he arrived late, as suited the occasion. Everyone jumped up and bowed with folded hands when he entered. Nirmala touched his feet and raised her hands to her forehead. Manohar brought a plate of sweets for the august visitor. After declining a couple of times Panditji yielded to the entreaties of Gomti and delicately picked a rasgulla with a thumb and two fingers of his right hand and quickly put it in his mouth before the juice could drip on his clothes. He wiped his fingers on a towel Nirmala held up to him, sat down and looked around. A hush fell on the courtyard. The children leaned on the rails to watch the proceedings. Every eye was on Panditji as he pulled out a scroll from an inside pocket in his vest. He did not unroll it; he did not need to. His eyes had a peculiar gleam as he focused on the baby. "This is the best horoscope I have seen in the fifty years I have been preparing them," he said in a slightly raised voice. After making sure it had sunk in he continued in a lower voice, "The planets were perfectly aligned at the moment of Ravi's birth and the evil Saturn was covered by holy Jupiter. Ravi has an exceptionally bright future in front of him. He will be a very successful lawyer or a doctor; he will travel all over the world and he will be admired by all who come across him. He will never be short of anything he needs. He will respect his elders and look after the juniors. You will all be proud of him but he will remain humble and ready to serve others."

Panditji's words sent a wave of excitement among the guests. They took turns holding the baby in their arms and looked admiringly at him once more before departing. Banwari Lal accompanied Panditji to the door and discretely passed him a roll of rupee notes which disappeared inside the vest. Nirmala took the scroll from Panditji and went to her room. She opened it and looked at every inch of the hyroglyphics with tears in her eyes. Behind the tears was the determination that no effort would be spared, no hardship would be too much to ensure that the predictions came true. The baby's cry brought her back to the present. She touched her forehead with the blessed horoscope before making room for it in her jewellery box. Only after locking the box and hiding the key under her clothes did she pick up the baby and put his mouth to her breast.

———◇◇———

Ravi was a healthy baby. He was growing quite well, started crawling at seven months and tried to stand up at ten months. Then one night his anguished cry woke Nirmala who was sleeping in a bed near his cot. His body was hot, he was having trouble breathing and sweat poured out of his tiny body. She wrapped the baby in a light blanket and held him tightly, trying to soothe his pain. For the rest of the night, the baby slept and cried in alternate spells of a few minutes. Nirmala walked, sat in a chair, laid down in bed but nothing helped the baby for long. Dr. Mitra was called. He examined the baby, diagnosed the illness as pneumonia, wrote a prescription and gave detailed instructions for his care. Just before leaving he looked at Ganesh and said, "Your wife will need all the help you can give her. Looking after a sick baby when there are three others to look after and another on the way is very hard. I know the maids are nowhere to be found these days. You will have to do as much as you can."

The fever lightened over the next two days. Then it became worse again. Ravi's temperature shot up to 105 and then it looked as if his breathing had stopped. Manohar rushed to the doctor and, to prepare for the worst, brought Panditji with him on his way back. Dr. Mitra arrived in his antique Morris Minor, looked anxiously at the baby, massaged his heaving chest and after a short while breathed the sigh of relief, "he will be all right. I will give you a new prescription. If the temperature does not go down below a hundred by the evening, send me a message." He scribbled on his pad, handed the sheet to Ganesh and rushed off to the next patient. He nodded to Panditji in the courtyard and told him with a faint smile, "The baby will be fine. Your services are not needed, at least for now." Indeed, Ravi came back from the death's door, recovered in a week and was soon crawling under every foot in the house.

Panditji was delighted that all was well even though his visit did not add to his hoard of rupee notes in a metal box hidden under the floor of his hovel. However, this loss was soon made up. He was needed twice within next six months. Nirmala's next baby, a girl named Soma, died when she was three months old. Nirmala was heartbroken. "I was so looking forward to having a daughter after four sons. We need a girl in the family, the boys need a sister," she cried. She had barely recovered when Rajesh, one year older than Ravi, got what Nirmala thought was diarrhea. It turned out to be cholera and he died after only two days of illness. The loss of two children was more than she could bear. Nirmala took to bed with fever. Kanaka came over from Aminabad to look after her daughter and the family. Ganesh respected his mother-in-law and appreciated her kindness to his family. On the other hand, he also knew of her dislike for him and kept out of her way as much as possible. It was a month before Kanaka, Ganesh and his parents could relax. In another couple of weeks Nirmala was well enough and Kanaka could return to her solitary existence. Before she left she took her daughter aside, made sure there were no snoopy ears nearby, and said, "You know you and the grandchildren are always welcome in Aminabad if they make your life miserable here."

Nirmala did not expect an offer like this and did not know what to make of it. Then the penny dropped and she blurted out, "I am not going anywhere without him. I married him for life, whatever turn it takes."

"A husband living with his wife's family becomes a laughing stock in the community. Surely you know that!" Kanaka said.

"Don't worry about him becoming a laughing stock, or any other stock. He won't go there. And without him I am not going anywhere."

"I might just as well tell you. I have no shoulders to lean on in my old age. I need to watch what I spend. I will do what I can for the schooling of my grandchildren. That is as far as I can go."

Ganesh noticed that the parting of his mother-in-law from her daughter was cool. But, wisely for a change, he kept the observation to himself.

2

Loss of a son and the only daughter as well as the family patriarch was only an introduction to Nirmala's misfortunes. Gomti fell apart altogether. She started drinking heavily and her outbursts became more frequent. She spent all her days upstairs by herself and sent the grandsons away if they went to see her. On her death Nirmala shared the grief of her husband as a dutiful wife would, but soon a feeling of relief took over. As for children, they forgot all the commotion in the house, grief of their parents or cremation ceremonies about their grandmother's passing on to her next life and only remembered being taken by Kiran's husband to a dhaba, traditional Indian restaurant where diners sit on a mat on the floor and are served chapattis and vegetable curry on banana leaves.

Among the neighbours was a family living in one corner of a dilapidated house next door. The only surviving child of the family was a boy named Vipda, Hindi word for distress. His father owned an ox-cart and earned his living by transporting items which were too big for a person to carry on his back. Vipda, his parents and the ox lived in a room with mud walls, a wood stove in the corner and mats on the dirt floor which served as chairs during the day and beds in the night. Ravi and Vipda were in the same class. They walked to school together and spent most of the evenings playing outside on the street. Nirmala often invited Vipda to join them for meals which he shyly did. Vipda dropped out of school after two years, his family moved away and was never seen again. This friend was the only student through twenty years of schooling who consistently outshone Ravi in studies. Nirmala had become fond of Vipda and was sorry when he left. On her visit to the temple the following Tuesday she prayed for Vipda to get an education and have a good life. However, she was well aware that in all likelihood he would end up driving an ox cart for a pittance like his father.

Rishi, Ravi's younger brother, was about three and a half when an accident happened that added much to the already stressful life of Nirmala. It must have been some festive occasion; Nirmala was preparing a feast. The stoves in the kitchen were being used for other dishes and Nirmala was using a spare stove in a corner of the courtyard to cook the rice. This was a small open stove which burned packed saw-dust. These stoves were unstable and dangerous but they were very popular in Ashapur because the sawdust was cheaper than coal or wood. The kids were sitting on the floor along the other wall in the courtyard eating their lunch. All of a sudden, Rishi stood up, moved towards the stove and said, "The pot is bubbling. Rice needs a good stir," Santosh saw Rishi picking up the ladle from the floor. He shouted, "Don't touch the pot." But Rishi did not listen and tried to push the ladle into rice. Three brothers looked in horror as the stove toppled over, overturning the pot and spilling rice and boiling water all over Rishi's legs. Nirmala heard the rattle and rushed out of the kitchen. Rishi was screaming in pain and his brothers were weeping in shock. Nirmala and Santosh moved Rishi to a bed. Dr. Mitra came over and cleaned the wounds. "The burns are serious, he will have to lie undisturbed for three months," he said after bandaging the legs. Then he added ominously, "Let us pray it does not have any long term effect."

The accident upset everyone in the family but no one more than Ganesh. He spent most of his time next to Rishi's bed, helping him turn when he needed to, helping him eat and drink and otherwise caring for him. When Rishi was awake he told him stories from the Hindu epics and when he was asleep he prayed for his rapid recovery. The wounds healed and he was walking again after five months. Dr. Mitra did not observe any other damage to Rishi's body.

From the ages of five to nine Ravi attended a boys' school founded by a Hindu reform movement for the sole purpose of promoting education; there were no religious classes or prayers. Santosh and Satya, and later Rishi, also went to this school. Older brothers were good students and active in sports and popular with teachers. Ravi was popular with the teachers too, except for one. While almost every one, teachers and students, wore loose cotton kurtas in a variety of colours and white pajama bottoms this teacher, known as Maulaviji, dressed in tight achkan, skin hugging cotton pants and a fez cap with black tail. He taught geography and punished Ravi harshly whenever he had the slightest excuse. On one occasion Maulaviji asked a boy in the back row, "What is the capital of Bombay?"

"Bombay sir," the reply was prompt.

"Good. What is the capital of Madras?" he asked a boy sitting in the front row.

"Madras, sir."

"Very good. What is the capital of Bengal, Ravi?"

Ravi was looking out of the window at the birds flying in intricate patterns. Startled, he said, "Bengal, sir,"

"Come here, you idiot. Look towards the children and bend down," Maulaviji commanded before picking up a bamboo cane from its perch beside the chalkboard. Ravi could not sit for rest of the day after that thrashing. The teacher sent a kid to fetch Santosh from his class and angrily described Ravi's behavious in front of all his class mates. Santosh added some flourishes of his own in relating the incident to Nirmala. Ravi stood before them looking at his toes with tears in his eyes.

"Is Bhaiya telling the truth?" Nirmala asked Ravi.

It was Santosh who answered, "Of course I am. He will jump ten feet if you touch his behind."

Trickle of tears became a flood, "I was looking at parrots flying around when Maulaviji asked me the question and a wrong answer jumped out of my mouth. He was cruel. I did not deserve such a hiding for such a small mistake."

Nirmala was not appeased, "Why would a boy be looking at parrots rather than attending to the teacher. You are a clever boy. You should be the best in the class. Promise me you will be the top student, now and always. Otherwise, I will add to the punishment too."

"I have learnt my lesson, Maaji. I want to be the best. I promise you that I will work hard and be at the top this year and every year. No more parrots for me," Ravi said putting his hand on his heart.

"O.K., come let me see how bad it is," Nirmala said lowering Ravi's pajamas. She rubbed Vaseline on the red spots. Whether it was the cream or tenderness of his mother, Ravi felt better straight away and ran out to find a friend to play with on the street.

These were difficult years for Nirmala. Bearing six children between the age of sixteen and twenty two, an alcoholic mother-in-law, a husband who never earned a penny and left it to her to provide the basic necessities, first by selling her jewelry and expensive saris, then by begging from her mother and other relatives, there was no end to stressful situations. What kept Nirmala going was the vision she had about her four sons, and a determination to make that vision a reality. She shielded the children as much as possible from daily vicissitudes and inspired them when they were older. The survival of the family in those years was all she could hope for. She was determined that she would achieve it.

3

The newly independent India got down to the job of settling nine million refugees from Pakistan. Mahatma Gandhi died on January 30, 1948 of the wounds from the bullets fired by a Hindu extremist. Jawaharlal Nehru became the undisputed leader of the country. Rapid industrialization under the state guidance became the government policy with the aim of removing poverty as soon as possible.

Shivanand had the customary reception at his home after his sister Gomti's cremation. The mood was somber and not much was said during the simple meal that was the custom on such occasions and was served on banana leaves instead of usual metal plates. After everyone's hands and faces were washed and dried, sister Parvati and brothers Yagni and Ganesh met with Shivanand and Sarla in Sarla's private chamber. Sarla called Nirmala and asked her to join the group. Yagni was in a hurry to come to the point and asked Shivanand directly, "Mamaji, you are the banker of our family. How much money and other assets are there to be divided among us?"

Shivanand did not need to look deep into his books for the answer, "There is a debit balance of a few hundred rupees in the account. As you know your mother was free with her money and only the best Scotch would do. The widow's pension after your Babaji's passing away was only fifty rupees and that doesn't buy even a week's supply. Babaji had left nine thousand rupees which lasted her till three months ago. You also know that much of her jewellery was stolen when you were children. Whatever is left should be in the safe and it goes to Parvati by Hindu law. The house now belongs to you brothers."

The suggestion upset Yagni and he raised his voice, "Ganesh has lived in the house for fifteen years free while I had to pay rent for my home. I think the whole house should now be mine to make up for it."

Sarla looked at Ganesh's distressed face, sensed a quiver go through her niece Nirmala and decided to take their side, "Ganesh and Nirmala did a lot for Gomti and Banwari too when he was alive. What they received and what they did balance out. The issue is not how to share but how to settle."

Yagni had his own idea, "I need as much money as I can get. There is a lot of money to be made in contracting government work if you have the seed money. My two sons are old enough to do the work as soon as they have enough to buy some equipment and hire some people."

Shivanand liked the idea and suggested what seemed to him an improvement, "You are right and the plan will work. I think you should include Ganesh in this business you are proposing."

Yagni was surprised but only for a moment. "The business will be barely big enough for two. Three will be one too many, at least for a while. Also it needs young bodies with a lot of energy. Ganesh won't fit in, I am afraid."

They knew what was meant and the subject was dropped. Shivanand picked up the baton again, "I can't see how Ganesh can pay you ten thousand rupees for half of the house. The only option is to sell it. Fortunately many of the refugees managed to escape with a lot of money and the market for large homes is quite hot right now. It will sell quickly if it is priced right. What will you do with your share Ganesh?"

Ganesh was not ready for important decisions. He stammered, "I don't know. I don't want to lose it all again as I did with my shop."

Shivanand knew what to do with money even if Ganesh did not, "I am building some houses on Rajpur Road. They cost about what your share will be. I will save one for you. You can move in there in a year."

It was Sarla's turn to be helpful, "There are two rooms empty above the servants' quarters. You can live there till your house is built."

Parvati also had an idea, "We know the owner of a car dealership in Kismatnagar. I will ask him if he has a job for Ganesh. I can't be sure but there is no harm in mentioning Ganesh to him. Every business man needs a manager he can trust."

Shivanand put Nirmala at ease, "If the job materializes and you move to Kismatnagar, you don't have to worry about your new house. It can be easily rented out for a hundred rupees a month."

Every thing settled at last, Sarla asked the servant to bring tea and snacks. The house was sold within a month and Ganesh's family moved into the rooms offered by Sarla just before the school year started. The rooms were small but there was a large verandah and the family was quite comfortable. The disruption in their lives was small and the boys could go to the same school as before. No one missed Gomti, and Nirmala was relieved that no was berating her at all hours of the day. She was hopeful that the job promised by Parvati would soon materialize and she wouldn't have to worry about how to feed the family.

---◇◇---

Almost a year had gone by. The year was 1949, almost two years after the independence. A great wave of optimism was sweeping the country. Big dams and huge factories were at various stages from planning to construction employing millions of workers. This activity pumped vast sums into communities which promoted the growth of small and medium size service and manufacturing businesses. Ganesh joined the wave when he received the good news. He was offered a minor supervisory job in the garage of Parvati's acquaintance for a hundred and twenty rupees a month. Nirmala saw this job as the end of her long struggle. To pay for the expenses of moving and settling down in Kismatnagar, Nirmala sent the last pieces of her jewelry, earrings and bangles, to Kiran and packed the family belongings in three cases. They took the overnight train to Kismatnagar in the third week of June. Although it was the monsoon season, the sky was clear and the morning bright when they got off the train.

Chand, Parvati's husband, was a retired Army officer and the scion of a prominent family of Kismatnagar. They lived off the income from inherited property. They had eight daughters and two sons. Six of the daughters were married to grooms from suitable families. The status of family demanded pompous weddings and big dowries for the daughters. Chand had to sell some of his property to meet the expenses of each wedding—and six weddings had taken their toll. Chand and Parvati were now reduced to a merely comfortable living although there were plenty of signs of the past glory. Their ancestral home, Chand Kutir, was spacious, located in the part of town once reserved for the bigwigs of the Raj. Their two adult sons and two teenage daughters lived with them. Two rooms on the upper floor were made available to Ganesh where they could have some privacy. There was space to set up a bathing area and a simple kitchen and they could use the toilets on the main floor. Here too, a large courtyard made up for the small rooms. The sons of Nirmala and Ganesh were admitted to the High School for Boys, conveniently located next door on property donated by the father of Chand.

Ganesh had only been on the job for a week when thirty garage workers, mechanics and their helpers, went on strike. Their demands were reasonable; overtime pay after eight hours at work, higher rates for public holidays and short breaks every two hours. The owners refused to negotiate and terminated the striking workers. Ganesh expressed the opinion to another supervisor that it was unreasonable not to negotiate. The colleague passed on the comment to the manager of the garage who called Ganesh to his office. It was a small room, no more than six square metres with cracks on the wall, one creaking wooden chair, a small table and a metal filing cabinet. The room reeked of the pungent smell of the cheap local cigarettes that the manager smoked every minute he was awake. He was short and fat, his dark face had several scars from injuries and his oily black hair was parted on the right to cover a bald patch. When Ganesh entered the room, the manager looked at his tall handsome figure for a long minute, made an effort to smile and asked, "How do you like working here, Ganeshji?"

"Manager sahib, I have only been here a few days. From what I have learned the job should be easy and enjoyable. Why do you ask?" Ganesh could sense that there was more than pleasantries behind the question.

"I don't like wasting time. So I will come to the point. Some supervisors have reported that you have been bad-mouthing the owners. Is this true?"

"Manager sahib, I am very grateful for the job and I have no reason to bad-mouth the people who will pay my salary. I did mention to one person my feeling that the workers' demands were not unreasonable and negotiation would have been helpful. That is just what I think. I am not going on strike to support them or anything like that."

The acknowledgement had the opposite response to what Ganesh had expected. The manager stood up knocking the chair back against the wall and shouted, "You are doing more harm by inciting others than you would do by going on strike. I can't have any supervisor in my garage who is not with the company with his whole heart. Pick up your tiffin box and get out of here. This company has no room for traitors. Consider yourself lucky that you are related to Chand Ji. Else I would be handing you over to the police. They show no mercy to ingrates like you."

Ganesh did not have the nerve to ask for the wages for the week he worked and slowly walked out wishing that a crack will open up and consume him. That was the last day Ganesh worked anywhere.

Nirmala was surprised to hear Ganesh's footsteps. She came out of the kitchen and was shattered by the look at his face. Ganesh told her the whole story and burst into tears, "I have disappointed you once again. I was so looking forward to proving to you that I am something. Now I know I am worthless."

Nirmala put her arm around his shoulders and tried to collect her thoughts. Ganesh continued, "Every one will think poorly of me and they will be right. It will be better for you if I were run over by the bus rather than live and add to your misery."

"Don't say silly things. I am indeed disappointed, but you were on the side of the poor and that is what the scriptures command us to do. We will manage somehow. The rent from our house in Ashapur will pay for the food and the school fees. Chand Jijaji will probably find you some other position.

Bhagwan has looked after us all these years. He will not forget us now."

"Jijaji's help did not work. Bhagwan is our last hope now."

"Calm down. You did what was right. I will make some tea and we will plan our next course of action."

The hopes of any help in finding a new job did not survive the afternoon. Parvati came upstairs an hour later. She brusquely refused Nirmala's offer of tea, took Ganesh aside and said, "The garage owner phoned your Jijaji to tell him the reasons of your dismissal. He is very angry and feels let down by you. He says he will never recommend you to any one again. You are on your own. I managed to calm him down a little. He has no problem with you living in these rooms for as long as you wish. But don't ask him for a reference when you apply for a job. And avoid coming face to face with him for a few days if you can."

Parvati saw her brother's grief-stricken face and hugged him. Knowing that words would not help him, she trudged down the steps leaning on the banister and stopped on the bottom step to dry her face with the corner of her white cotton sari before entering the kitchen to issue instructions to the cook.

4

Jamna, an old woman, came to wash dishes in the evening. She noticed immediately that something was wrong. Nirmala did not respond to her greeting and there was a lot of food left on two dishes.The children were quarrelling rather than doing their homework. The situation became clear when she had finished her work. Nirmala came over, handed her a five rupee note and bluntly told her that she was not needed any more. Jamna was shocked, "Why, am I being terminated Maaji? Is my work not good enough?"

Nirmala did not know how to answer her without revealing the truth so she simply said, "Jamna, I am sorry, but Babuji lost his job today and we can not afford to pay you. When he has found another job I will contact you. Till then I will have to do the dishes."

Jamna tried to touch Nirmala's feet but Nirmala moved away.

The next morning it was Ravi's turn to go to the front of the house where the milkman milked his cow directly into the customers' pots. Nirmala handed him the smaller pot. "Tell Madhav that we will need only one pint every morning. No need to tell him about your Pitaji's job. Be careful and do not spill any."

The children noticed that their glass of milk was half full but did not complain. The chapatis left over from the previous night made up for the missing milk. Nirmala made the tea with fewer leaves and added half the usual amount of milk and sugar. Ganesh swallowed hard and did not complain.

Nirmala cleaned the kitchen, had a bath and walked over to the temple about a mile away. It was only her second visit and she had not made any friends yet but prayer gave her solace and hope. On the way back she stopped by at her favourite fruit and vegetable stall, picked eight medium sized potatoes and handed them to the seller. He weighed them.

"Bibiji, one rupee, four annas. Will you like some carrots, just pulled them out this morning? And bananas, perfectly ripe?"

Nirmala felt weak in her knees but pulled herself together, "No I don't need the carrots or the bananas or anything else. And these potatoes should only be one rupee. Since when do eight potatoes cost more than a rupee?"

"Bibiji, you are a regular. You know that you get six small potatoes for a rupee. I have already given you a special discount. I don't want to insult you by offering you an anna but a rupee for these potatoes—no it is not possible."

"OK, take one out and give me the rest for a rupee. That is not such a big deal, is it?"

"Bibiji, it takes my profit away but I will do it for you."

Nirmala kept her face down when she handed him her bag and a rupee. She hurriedly walked away and slowed down only when she came to the steps leading to her rooms. The children would soon be home for lunch. She took two potatoes out and started peeling them to make potato pancakes.

After the children had returned to school, she got the laundry out. Five shirts, five trousers, underwear, her cotton sari, blouse, three towels and a handkerchief; it made a big heap. She checked the pockets and found scraps of paper and odd coins. She sat down on a low wooden stool next to the tap, filled the bucket and started washing the clothes one by one. The younger children's clothes were really dirty and needed an extra wash. After the dirty heap had moved from left to right as a clean heap, she squeezed the water out by twisting the clothes and hung them to dry in the hot sun. The washing took more than an hour but it saved the rupee Manji, the washer woman, would have charged. Another plus, Manji beat the clothes against the floor and so the clothes wore out faster.

Washing done, Nirmala saw her shadow and estimated that she had an hour before children came home from school. She picked up a magazine and had just sat down on the bed when Ganesh finished his afternoon prayer. He stood up, stretched his limbs and lit a cigarette.

"Is the tea ready?" he asked.

Nirmala looked up, "I have so many things to do now, what with dishes and clothes, your tea completely slipped my mind. Let me rest my legs for a minute."

Ganesh did not sound pleased, "You know I like tea with my cigarette after the prayer. This is the only luxury I still allow myself."

"I did not realize five minutes mattered so much." Nirmala muttered on her way to the kitchen. Half way there she turned around and added, "You could learn to prepare tea too so you do not have to depend on me."

Ganesh followed her and watched her light the little stove, place measured amounts of tea, sugar, milk and water in a pan and bring it to boil. He observed how she removed the lid just before the mixture came to boil and let it simmer for five minutes. She poured the tea in a brass mug and handed to him. He took a sip and pulled a face, "It tastes like dish water. It needs more tea, milk and sugar."

"I need the milk for the children and the tea and sugar have to last a week. We have to get used to this tea. When you have found a job we will have proper tea, till then this is all we can afford."

The arrow hit home. Ganesh finished the drink and cigarette in silence and went out without a word. Nirmala was sorry her words hurt his feelings and told herself "I must watch my tongue when my body is aching."

5

After leaving Nirmala, Ganesh walked the long driveway of Chand Kutir, turned left on the Cantonment Road towards the Polo Ground. No one remembered any game of polo being played there since before the war but the name had stuck. Every evening and during the afternoon on Sundays older children played soccer, field hockey, volley ball and cricket, and tiny tots ran around shouting incomprehensible words in between the players. The rest of the time, it was the place for unemployed men to sit on the scattered benches or squat on the grass whiling away the time, contemplating the present and dreading the future. In the far corner, someone had erected a human-size concrete statue which could be, by some stretch of imagination, that of Hanuman the 'monkey god'. Devotees put flowers at its feet, garlands around its neck, painted saffron lines on its forehead and sometimes left sweets for their Lord. Ganesh had not noticed this idol of his favourite diety before, but the turmoil in his head now guided him to this simple place of worship.

Ganesh sat on the ground in front of the idol and chanted verses which glorified Hanuman's heroic deeds, merciful nature and everlasting kindness to his devotees. Ganesh emphasized his own humility and utter dependence on Hanuman's mercy and prayed that his family would be looked after. When Ganesh finished after half an hour or so he felt assured that his troubles were ephemeral and peace descended on him.

The children came home from school, drank the watered milk, shared the leftover chapatis and ran off to play with their new friends from school. Nirmala sat down and wrote a letter to Kanaka in Aminabad conveying the bad news. She knew that her mother's heart had no soft spot for Ganesh and therefore she went to extreme lengths to defend him and blame the company. In spite of fifteen years of relentless hardship due largely to his ineptness, she felt compelled to present his best image to her mother. On her way to the mailbox she ran into Parvati who answered her greeting with "If you are not in a hurry I have something I need to mention to you."

"Jiji, why would I be in a hurry when you want to speak to me? Is every thing all right? Have children been bothering you?

"Children will be children.My nephews are a joy to have around. Ganga Bhabi called this morning. She was anxious about Ganesh and the family. You have been here more than a month and they haven't seen you. Yagni Bhai is the head of our family, we owe him some respect. You should call on them soon."

"Jiji, we feel a little uncomfortable after what happened after Mataji left us." Referring to her husband as 'he' according to the custom of the day she continued, "He thinks that Bhaiji does not want to have anything to do with his poor kid brother. Now that he has lost his job, he feels even more hesitant. He doesn't want to look as if he is begging for help."

"Don't be foolish. Yagni Bhai is headstrong and says things which should not be said. But Ganga loves you all and is particularly hurt at your neglect. Think about it. In any case asking for help from a brother it is not begging."

"Jiji, you are right. I should have called on them on my way back from the temple. I will do it this week."

The following Saturday, Nirmala shortened her prayer at the temple and took a small detour on her way back to Yagni and Ganga's house. She knew the location but had never been there before. She was surprised at the size of the bungalow that matched the address. It was set well back from the road. The grounds were reasonably well maintained even though the grass had mostly died in the summer heat. The large porch was freshly painted in light blue and led to an impressive entrance.When Nirmala knocked, a servant came to the door and led her to a patio through a wide passage with well-appointed rooms on each side. The patio opened on a square patch of lawn which had greener grass than that in the front and had swings and slides for the children to play on. Nirmala was pleased at these signs of her brother-in-law's prosperity. Ganga entered from a door on the left, a marble image of Lord Mahavir was visible behind her. Nirmala bent down to touch her sister-in-law's feet but Ganga pulled her up and guided her to a divan with fresh white sheets and sausage-shaped pillows with Batik covers. She sat down next to her and said, "I am so happy to see you. What kept you away for so long? Now you have to tell me everything. Parvati told me about Ganesh's job but I want to hear it from you."

Ganga's empathy broke down Nirmala's reserve and her frustration spilled over. She told the story in an angry tone, angry with her fate, not with any individual, certainly not her husband. She added, "We will manage somehow. The rent from our house in Ashapur is enough for our daily needs. The school is next door and the children do not need much. 'He' is looking for another job. It is very hard without any connections; he doesn't even know where to look. But I sometimes think that his heart is not in it. I do not know whether we will stay here after the end of the school year if he does not find something."

"God's will is supreme. God takes care of His devotees. You must put your faith in Him," Ganga consoled her but did not offer financial help. She did invite Nirmala and the family to visit whenever it was convenient. She insisted that the family come for dinner the following day till Nirmala ran out of excuses. It was now time to be home for lunch and Nirmala took her leave. She reviewed the visit on her way home, felt good about it overall and decided that it was time to forget the harsh words said by Yagni after Gomti's funeral.

Other than the families of Ganesh's siblings they did not have any friends in Kismatnagar and their constrained financial situation severely limited the means by which they could develop new contacts. A visit to Yagni and Ganga was, therefore, a welcome respite. The children enjoyed these visits not only because the cousins were of similar ages and great play-mates but also because the food had variety and they had a choice of juices to drink rather than watered-down milk. Nirmala was glad that the boys got a good meal even though it was not an altogether pleasant feeling to observe them greedily demolishing every dish that was served.

From all outward appearances Nirmala was coping very well with the difficult situation they were in. She laughed at Ganesh's jokes, played card games with children after they finished the home work, even appreciated the tea Ganesh now made several times every day. But the veneer came off suddenly one evening. Nirmala was sitting on a low stool with dirty dishes all around her. The bucket of water was a few feet from her. Ganesh happened to be going by. "Will you move that bucket for me, dear?" she asked. Ganesh disregarded the request; perhaps he did not hear it. Something snapped in Nirmala, tears started streaming down her cheeks.

"When I was growing up men were not expected to help with housework. They were supposed to enter the kitchen only to eat. But they worked hard to support the family. They didn't spend the day praying to Lord Hanuman at the Polo Ground or lazing around the house polluting it with their foul cigarette smoke. I am left with all the chores. Only a blind man would not see that I need help. All these able bodied men around me, they can see how tired I am after all the cooking, washing, cleaning and shopping but not one lifts a finger to help. The constant anxiety about money is killing me. Since the day I left my mother's home, I have had to worry about where the next meal is to come from. And will be doing it till the day I die. I hate my situation, I hate it and there is no shoulder for me to cry on."

She spoke so loud that Parvati heard her from downstairs, although Nirmala would have been mortified if she realized it. She carried on until the chores were done. Then she lay down sobbing on the bed until she fell asleep.

When she woke up she acted as if nothing had happened. Everyone in the household was relieved and things returned to normal. If the idea of taking over some of the washing and cleaning jobs had occured to any of the males, it was quickly forgotten.

The event did not eliminate the build up of stress. It built up again almost every week and then Nirmala would blow up, usually in the afternoon, when she was doing the dishes or washing the clothes. Tears streamed down her puffy cheeks, her hair became disheveled, and the words fell out of her mouth whether there was any one in earshot or not. Once in a while, she would hit her head against the wall hard enough to cause bumps. Ganesh, and any of the boys who were there, looked on helplessly and did not know how to console her. It was truly disconcerting to them If they tried to stop her she pushed them back, "Don't come near me. If you really wanted my welfare, you would offer to help. Any one who can eat should be able to cook. Any one who wears clothes should be able to wash. But not my husband and not my sons. They have an unpaid servant to do all their dirty work. From princess to a maid, that is my fate. Go away, leave me to my work. Come back when it is time to eat. I will live with my misery and there is no one who can help me. The sins of past lives are for me to amend and I will do it without any help, thank you."

Ganesh did feel anxiety and guilt due to the financial hardship being caused by his inability to find a job but he did not show it. He kept aloof from the family affairs and did not really have much to do with his sons. If there were any decisions to be made, he left them for Nirmala. The children went to their mother when they had some news or needed something. Pitaji was someone who was to be treated with respect but generally ignored.

6

The boys made friends easily and spent much of their time playing at Polo Ground or at their friends' homes when the weather was inclement. It didn't appear long to them before the final examinations arrived. While the children prepared for exams, their parents had to decide whether they wanted to stay put or return to Ashapur. As Nirmala had anticipated, Ganesh's feeble attempts to find work were not successful and he had given up. Ganesh had his siblings in Kismatnagar but Nirmala's friends and most of her relations were in Ashapur. Moreover, travel to Aminabad from Kismatnagar was arduous and expensive and Nirmala missed her mother. After the formality of discussions with Parvati and Yagni, the decision to move back was made. They packed their few possessions once more and took the train to Ashapur. Parting between Ganesh and Parvati was heart rending for both—Parvati felt some guilt for not being able to help him and Ganesh knew he had let her down.

While it had been a difficult year for the parents, the children had reasons to remember the year with some fondness. The school was close and the teachers were especially considerate to the family of the founder. The brothers were well-behaved as well as bright students and that helped. Nirmala remembered one particular incident from this year with some fondness. Although youngest in the class and smaller than most of his classmates, Ravi was appointed the 'monitor' of the class. The job of the monitor was to keep order in the class when teacher was away. He made a list of names of unruly classmates and gave it to the teacher on his return. Corporal punishment was legal in those days and the fear of swollen palms and buttocks kept the class in order. To be on the safe side, bigger and rowdier boys bribed Ravi with ripe tamarind from trees that lined the roads circling the polo ground. It worked because he loved to suck the fruit and Nirmala made a wonderful sauce with what he took home. One memorable afternoon, however, the boys were restive and the list grew to include almost every student. Ravi was so disappointed with his failure that before handing the list to the teacher, he added his name to it. The teacher looked at the list, smiled and limited his punishment to a mild tongue lashing.

The family moved back to the rooms they had occupied in Shivanand's mansion before their hopeful journey. Sarla was sorry for Nirmala's plight and offered to have Ravi live with her for a year. Nirmala had reservations but she accepted the offer in order to reduce the financial burden. For some years Sarla, Naniji and Ravi, lived in a large bungalow located about two miles from the downtown area of Ashapur, apart from her husband. The old gentleman lived in his downtown mini-castle separate from both of his wives. Naniji was a short, frail lady of very respectable demeanour, rather old for her fifty years. Two adult sons lived with her. Vijay, in his thirties, was married and occupied three large rooms with his wife and two daughters aged seven and five. Rajneesh, just turned twenty one, was preparing to leave for England to follow the illustrious footsteps of his father who had studied law at Oxford. Two distant rich relatives lived as paying guests of Sarla in a cottage located on the property and joined the rest for all their meals. In all, with various servants and those served, about fifteen people lived there.

Ravi's status in the household was much above that of a servant though not quite that of a member of the family. Thanks to the prediction of Panditji based on the horoscope, Ravi was thought of as a promising boy who would grow to be a successful doctor or a lawyer. This allowed him some privileges and many kindnesses were bestowed on him, not only by Naniji but other relatives as well. For starters, within the first few days of his moving in, Naniji gave him new sets of clothes and shoes, not fancy like the children of Vijay's family would wear but utilitarian as suited his station of a poor relative. He ate with the relatives, although he was not expected to speak unless spoken to. Initially, his bed was a small string cot in the store room. However, when Rajneesh departed for England, he was allowed to move into his luxurious suite with a large spring bed.

One afternoon Sarla was resting in her bed. Ravi was off from school that day. He came in, sat down next to her feet and asked, "Naniji, are you well?"

"I am well other than a little headache. I think it will go away after some rest," Sarala replied.

"Will it help if I massaged it a little."

"Oh. That will be wonderful," Sarla said, more to please him than her need.

Ravi moved a chair near the top of the bed and massaged her head for a few minutes. "You are a good massage boy. My headache is gone. Can you massage my feet now," Sarla asked.

Ravi returned to his previous position at the foot of the bed and massaged her feet and lower legs. He stopped when he heard gentle snoring a few minutes later and crept away.

Naniji called him at tea time and gave him a rupee, his reward for a good job. Massaging Naniji became his afternoon job on days off from school and the rupee he received was his weekly allowance.

Ravi went to the American Presbyterian Mission School for boys. It was located in the centre of the city, a block from his parents and Shivanand. During the half hour bible class every morning a Christian teacher read passages from the Bible. Ravi had good-natured arguments with the teachers almost every day in the same spirit that he debated with Hindu preachers. Realizing that his questions were well-intentioned and guided by curiosity, not by mean-spirited religious bias, the teachers indulged him.

There was no public transportation in the town at that time. The paying guest relatives left for work about the same time as Ravi did for school and often gave him a ride in their car to a point where their paths diverged. He walked the remaining half mile and the whole two miles on the way back. He went to Shivanand's kitchen for lunch but never saw the patriarch. Which is just as well because he, like every one else, was in awe of him. Ravi did see Shivanand one evening a week when he visited his family at the bungalow. He invariably brought Cadbury's milk chocolates for his granddaughters but never anything for Ravi. Ravi did not expect to be treated the same as his cousins and therefore, did not feel put down. His disappointment, if he felt any, was mitigated by the cousins sharing the treats with him on instructions of their parents.

One hot afternoon Ravi was roaming barefoot in the bungalow enjoying the cold sensation of the marble floor on the soles of his feet. The family was sitting in the living room laughing at the strange behaviour of a European family living in the neighbourhood. Vijay noticed Ravi's unshod feet and shouted, "Ravi—bare feet." The scorn in the tone touched a sensitive nerve in Ravi. He burst into tears and ran to his room. Lakshmi, Vijay's wife, followed Ravi, held him in a tight embrace till he stopped sobbing. She wiped his face with the corner of her silk sari, "Wait here for a minute, I will be back," she said leaving the room. She returned with half of a bar of chocolate and Ravi's glistening eyes smiled in thanks. Vijay often mentioned that incident to point out his nephew's unreasonable sensitivity, while Ravi remembered it as a sign of discomfort in his situation. He was too young to understand that Vijay's remark was far from malicious. It was intended to make him aware that only the servants went barefoot.

The two girls played with Ravi once in a while but he was too young to notice that he did not receive the respect due to an older male cousin. This infrequent association came to an abrupt halt towards the end of his stay. In the extensive, but rather unkempt grounds at the back, front lawn was always immaculate, there was a prolific bush of Chinese gooseberries. The ripe fruit was a golden ball about one centimeter in diameter which hung from the branch covered by a pair of leaves. Nobody had any idea how it got there but the fruit was delicious. Vijay loved the plant and watered it daily, summer or winter, with a small watering can, much to the chagrin of the gardener whose job it was. Ravi developed the habit of picking out the fruit and leaving the cover around the fruit intact, it was easier than breaking off the stem. The two girls saw him do it and started doing it too. Soon, the fruit was all gone but the bush still appeared loaded to Vijay when he dutifully watered it. One afternoon, Maharaja and Maharani of Pipalpur were visiting Vijay and Lakshmi. After a few drinks Vijay said to Maharani, "I will show you a bush with delectable fruit. I am not even sure what it is called. Gardener tells me it is imported from China." While Lakshmo poured another scotch on the ice cubes for the Maharaja, Vijay guided Maharani to the bush, "Go on pick a fruit and taste it." Maharani obliged but there was no fruit under the cover. She tried again and again. Vijay's brown face turned redder and redder. He turned to his daughters watching them from a distance, "Do you know who picked all my fruit?"

"Ravi did," they replied in unison pointing to Ravi hiding behind Sarla some distance away.

Maharani saw the humour in the incident. She laughed, turned towards the house and said, "Don't be mad with the playful boy, Vijay. I am sure the fruit is as wonderful as you said. I can smell it in the bush. I can wait till next season to taste it."

In view of the incident of a few days ago Vijay limited the punishment to a well-directed frown and a word with Sarla. Even though Ravi accepted all the blame, the two cousins never came close to him again. The final blow was delivered a few weeks after returning to his parents. He gave a doll to one of them on her birthday. "I have so many beautiful dolls, what will I do with this ugly one in cotton clothes," she responded with the contempt the gift or its giver did not deserve.

Just when Ravi's year with Naniji was nearing its end the family had a lucky break. Satto, the older brother of Kanaka, had a large home in Ashapur. He was transferred to Delhi and offered Nirmala the use of a part of the house in his absence in return for the caretaker duties. The family now had three rooms with a separate kitchen, a courtyard and storage room. There was the front yard where the children could play badminton and there were neighbourhood kids they could join in games of cricket on the unpaved street. Ravi moved there after the end of the school year. He was happy to be back with his family even though he did not get the weekly rupee and meals were frugal. Now he had brothers to fight with, friends to play with and the school was only half a mile away.

The year with Naniji was the most formative year in Ravi's childhood. Some of his good and bad personality traits were formulated then. He found out what an emotional roller coaster being a poor relation in a prosperous clan was.

During that year he vowed that when he was an adult, people would look up to him, not down upon him, and his wife and children would not need to look elsewhere for support. He also developed an unhealthy respect for money and for those who have it, unhealthy because he craved the respect which is accorded to the rich and the powerful, and in later life was often overcome with disappointment for not having received what he considered was his due.

If the year with the rich relatives had unpleasant memories, it was not Sarla's fault. She loved Ravi, was kind to him and had good intentions. Later, she provided crucial financial support to supplement his scholarships through his five years at the University. Ravi never verbally expressed his gratitude for her kindness; she would have been embarrassed had he done so.

This was also the year Santosh finished high school. Sarla sent a servant to Nirmala asking her to come over for tea and bring Santosh along. After the butler had served tea and gulab jamuns, Sarla handed Santosh some ten rupee notes and said, "Here is a reward for finishing school. Get some new clothes made. Tell me how did you do in your exams?"

"Naniji, most of the papers were easy. I had some trouble with English but I think I should get more than fifty percent."

"What kind of jobs are you applying for now?"

"Naniji, I want to go to college and do B.A. before working. If I get first class I may go on to do M.A. and then apply for some Indian Administrative Service."

"Have you talked it over with Ganesh and Nirmala? They need an income as soon as possible. I suggest you apply for a job in the municipality. Nanaji's recommendation will work for you there."

It was time for Nirmala to respond, "Mausiji, I have had the burden of an uneducated husband all my life. I hope that my sons will remove that burden; but not before they are ready. I want them to go to college, take their degrees and then apply for jobs that will bring us credit. I don't want my sons to be clerks who can be thrown out at the slightest whim of the officers. I want them to be officers. Their father has the same view. We will manage somehow for a few more years. Bhagwan will look after us as He has for all these years of hardship."

Sarla knew her niece and was not surprised by this response. Still, there was coolness in the air for rest of the visit.

This set the family pattern and other sons proceeded on the assumption that they would go to college. To keep the family afloat, Kanaka sold the little property Umrao had left her, and Sarla helped when the needs were dire. The children's clothes were worn out, but never dirty. They always had books even though they were bought used, and pencils were discarded only when they could not be gripped any more. Kanaka's money ran out when Santosh was in his final year. The financial situation now became desperate.

7

Rajesh was an acquaintance of Ganesh from their school days although recent contact had been minimal. At school he was a short, thin boy with thick horn rimmed glasses, a geek secretly envious of the boys who were good in sports. He helped Ganesh with home work. However, Ganesh had no time for him in non-school matters. Rajesh went on to become a dentist and had a flourishing practice till the the independence when British administrators and army officers left and his clientele considerably thinned. So when Satya appeared in his clinic with a toothache he was happy to examine his mouth without asking to be paid in advance as was his normal practice. He found six cavities and filled them. Ravi was in his chair the day after Satya was finished. He had only four cavities but they were deeper and needed more work. After finishing this work he prepared a detailed invoice and mailed it to Ganesh.

There was no payment in the return post. Or at the end of the month. Rajesh sent a reminder advising that 2% interest would be added if payment was not received by the end of the next month. He did that for three months and then called on Ganesh one evening. Nirmala greeted him warmly, "Doctor sahib, I am so happy to see you. I am sorry Ganesh is not back from the temple. Will you like some tea or some lemonade?"

"Bhabi, thank you but I have to get back. I was passing by and it struck me to check if you had received my bills. It has been several months now and you could help me greatly by settling the account."

"Rajesh Ji, we did get the bill and I apologize for not getting in touch with you. We would have settled the account if we could. The truth is that we are even having trouble paying the school fees. I do not really know what to tell you."

"Bhabi I am sorry to hear about your predicament. Can you give me some idea when I should expect at least some of the money?"

"I wish I could answer that. I will not lie to you. Amma can't help us any more and I have no idea how I will feed the family next month. We will pay you, with interest, but I can't say it will be soon."

Dr. Rajesh Devta D.D.S. was too civil to say anything unpleasant to the wife of his childhood hero. He mumbled, "Please see what you can do to help," and departed.

———◇◇———

During dinner Rajesh mentioned to his wife the plight of Ganesh and the unpaid bill. Her response was prompt, "You will do your old friend a favour by informing Shivanand of his nephew's precarious state and his debt. If our bill gets paid in the process so much the better."

"What a wonderful idea. Why didn't I think of it? I will broach the subject next time he is in the chair. He should be visiting soon."

Four weeks later a servant brought a verbal message to Ganesh, "Bara Sahib wants to see you this afternoon in his office." Ganesh, surprised, asked the servant "Do you know why he wants me? Why in the office?"

"Sahib is very angry. I do not know why. Be ready for a long lecture," the servant confided and trundled off.

Shivanand was looking at some papers when Munimji, the bookkeeper who doubled as a receptionist, directed Ganesh into his presence. Shivanand did not look up for ages, leaving Ganesh nervously fidgeting in front of him. At last he raised his eyes in a dreadfully slow motion. He stared at his nephew's face for a full minute. Then he spoke one syllable at a time, softly at first, then raising the voice in measured steps "Why do I have to hear of your problems in my dentist's chair? Why do I have shopkeepers visiting me about your debts? Why do you buy if you can't pay?"

Shivanand paused to take a breath, he was screaming now, "Tell me, once and for all. Why, why, why would any one with any brain do that? You do have some left in your head, don't you?"

Ganesh was startled. He never imagined that the geek Devta would babble his affairs to the family patriarch. Who else had been coming here without his knowledge? Shivanand's glare was scorching his face he had to say something.

"Mamaji, the rent from the house does not last even two weeks now that the children are older. Amma has stopped helping us. May be she can't. We live as frugally as we can."

"How do you intend to pay these debts? Your sons can't pay them for you. What they earn will be barely enough for them. Do you have any ideas?"

"Mamaji, Nirmala and I are at our wit's end. We spend all our days praying and nights worrying but we can't think of any way out."

"Well, I can think one way out. It will solve your problem for now but may leave you stranded later. I will sell your rental house and settle your debts with the proceeds. A few thousand rupees may be left. You can use them to start a business. I am building some shops and you can rent one if you know what sort of business you can manage."

With that statement, Shivanand's eyes returned to the papers. Ganesh took the clue, bowed with folded hands and turned around to leave.

"Let Munimji know when you have decided about renting the shop," Ganesh received Shivanand's final instruction.

Two months later Ganesh received a note from Shivanand. It was short and to the point. "The house built from the proceeds of your family home was sold. After paying your creditors, a sum of 5,143 rupees is left in your account. I trust you will use it wisely to set up a business and not in daily expenses of your family."

Shivanand's trust was misplaced. No one will ever know for certain whether Ganesh had the skill to operate a business, he certainly did not have the nerve to start one. Fear of failure stopped him from doing anything at all, whether constructive or destructive. Nirmala knew that there was nothing to be gained by pushing her husband and planned to use the money carefully for the necessities and make it last for at least a couple of years.

During the nineteen fifties all levels of government were encouraging industry, small and large. Entrepreneurs were scraping together every rupee and setting up factories to build everything from humble pins and needles to tractors and trucks. Colleges were being built all over the country to train engineers to run the industry. If you had the connections to get the permits and knew who to bribe to get the grants, Lakshmi, the goddess of prosperity, was at your service. If you did not have either of these, but were a bright student, you could train to be a professional. Others could go to local colleges to receive appropriate training for a variety of jobs that paid barely enough to feed and clothe the family.

Santosh qualified as a teacher and accepted a position in a village school six hours by bus from Ashapur. His salary was the princely sum of one hundred and forty rupees. Three days after the end of the month Nirmala received a money order for sixty rupees. "You must look after yourself. Make sure you are eating well and have comfortable living accommodation. I do not wish to deprive you for our needs," she wrote to him.

"I am comfortable and you do not need to worry about me. It is very quiet here, lot of time to read and write. I spend most of my spare time on walks in the fields and on writing essays on village life," he replied by return mail.

Nirmala was relieved by his assurance and thanked Lord Mahavir every month when the money order for similar amount arrived.

A year later, Satya graduated with a Master of Commerce degree and joined the officer cadre in the auxiliary services of the Indian Air Force. Santosh found teaching unrewarding and obtained a position in the Indian Civil Service which paid enough for a family to live on in comfort, had a pension scheme and still left time to write. Nirmala felt that her battles were almost over now that two of her sons were well settled. Sarla was happy to be proven wrong and told Kanaka next time she was in Aminabad how proud she was of what Nirmala had done for her sons and how well they had turned out.

Nirmala knew that her work was not done yet. She had even higher hopes from the younger two who excelled in science and could qualify in the coveted professions of engineering or medicine. Her financial situation was not any better though. While she was getting some support from her employed sons, the account set up by Shivanand was exhausted and debts were beginning to pile up again.

Rishi had been a delicate boy since the stove accident in his early childhood days which had caused extensive burns all over her body. He caught colds easily and regularly suffered from aches and pains. He was very thin and several inches taller than his brothers. Around this time he started growing even taller and ran out of breath after the slightest exertion. Nirmala suspected something was wrong. Dr. Mitra examined him and told her that his heart was growing larger. He had no cure for it; there was a possibility that the problem would fix itself. Nirmala had more on her plate than she could handle and took the old doctor's words at face value and Rishi's health did not get the attention it deserved. If Nirmala suspected that the old doctor was only consoling her because he knew that she did not have the means to do much about it at that time, she kept it to herself. There was someone else that needed her attention and he couldn't wait.

Ravi had been her favourite son since that day sixteen years ago when Panditji read his horoscope. He had lived up to everyone's expectation. He had grown to be of medium height, had a fair complexion with dark wavy hair, always top of the class, polite to elders, confident but not vain, and popular with young and old alike. Nirmala always looked at Ravi as her salvation. He would grow up, be a great doctor or an engineer, earn more than enough to pay off their debts and enable her to spend her old age traveling to holy places and helping those in need. Now he was sixteen, ready to enter a professional college. She encouraged him to take the entrance tests to several elite engineering colleges all over India without having any idea of the cost involved.

Two months after the tests Ravi received the acceptance letters from the two most prominent colleges. He was thrilled. And with good reason; he was one of only three hundred selected from twenty thousand applicants, many of them with two or three years of extra schooling. Of the two schools, his choice was the one set up by MIT, the celebrated American institution. Indian Institute of Technology, IIT for short, was located near Calcutta one thousand miles and forty hours of train journey away. The letter of acceptance detailed the expected costs of tuition, residence and minimum pocket expenses; at least one hundred and twenty five rupees a month and another five hundred per year for travel and books. Ravi read the letter to Ganesh and Nirmala with great delight. Though delighted with the great news, they were shocked by the cost estimates. They sat with heads in their hands; watching the curtain of two thousand rupees a year fall on their hopes.

After the excitement died down, Ravi read the attachment detailing facilities available at the institute. The third and last page mentioned scholarships available to the new students. A scholarship examination would be held in Physics, Chemistry, Mathematics and Drawing a month after the start of the term. The top 32 entrants would receive a merit scholarship of seventy five rupees per month renewable every year based on their performance. Another 32 of the remaining students would receive merit-cum-poverty scholarship of sixty rupees if they could prove the financial need. This provided the ray of hope Nirmala was desperate for. She traveled to Aminabad and Kanaka agreed to give her five hundred rupees for travel and first two months and twenty five rupees a month thereafter. Ravi could stay if he got a scholarship, otherwise he would return and go to local college for a science degree. Nirmala drafted a letter for Kanaka to send to Sarla asking if she could help in some way.

When Nirmala returned home Ravi greeted her with "Naniji wants to see you and me as soon as possible. She is very angry, it seems."

"Well, let's go. We can't have Mausiji angry," Nirmala said to Ravi.

"I have tea ready for you. Drink it before you go. You are tired after the journey. It will refresh you," Ganesh intercepted.

"That is very thoughtful of you. But I have no time for tea. We need her help and she has to be pacified. Come on Ravi," Nirmala commanded.

———◊◊———

Sarla was indeed furious, "Why do I have to hear from my poor sister what I should have been told by you? Rush off to Aminabad without sending me a message and I lose my sleep dreading if my sister is dying. Then I get a letter with all the good news. Why couldn't any one tell me herself? Why didn't you rush here to tell me Ravi? Am I not the Naniji who has doted on you since you were born? Was I not the person praying for you when you were given up for dead as a baby? Will someone tell me what I have done to be tortured like this by the niece and her son I have looked after like my own progeny?"

When the storm abated Ravi bent down and touched Sarla's feet like a penitent and murmured, "I am sorry, I should have come straight away. Pitaji thought that it was not good to make a fuss till Maaji had seen Amma because without her support I won't be able to go anyway. It is my mistake. Please forgive me. Next time there is any news you will be the first one to hear."

Sarla was mollified somewhat, "OK, now that you explain it I understand. Kanaka's plan does change things and gives us a ray of hope. You know what I'll do? You get the merit scholarship and I'll give you the scholarship to make up the difference. Does that make every one happy? And yes. Don't mention it to any one. Ravi is a special case. I don't want every relation to come asking me for scholarship. I will write to Kanaka myself."

If sixteen-year-old Ravi felt the pressure to prove that he was crème de la crème in a country of 400,000,000 people he did not show it. He told those who asked that he was delighted at the opportunity and felt certain that he would succeed. It was the hottest time of the year when he stood against the wall of a third class compartment carrying forty people, twice the number of seats. After thirty eight hours in train and an hour on a bicycle rikshaw he arrived at the hostel to which he was assigned.

9

Dr. B.S. Jain, a young lecturer in Philosophy and Ethics, had the job of checking the tally of final marks after the scholarship examination. There was a card for each student on which clerks had penciled the marks for each subject. Dr. Jain was to check each card against alphabetical lists for each subject, total all marks on the card and arrange them in order of total mark on the card. Lists for each subject were arranged side by side on his desk just above the stack of cards also in alphabetical order. Clerks had done an excellent job and he did not find a mistake till he reached a strange entry. It had two marks in the nineties, one eighty eight and the last one, for Drawing, a measly single digit. He was further struck by the name on the card, same surname as his own but not someone he knew. It did not seem right that someone from his community with outstanding scores in three subjects should have such a poor score in the fourth. He had no hesitation in correcting the anomaly by a simple expedient of adding 8 behind the lonely digit, on the card as well as on the sheet. Totaling four two digit numbers in his head was an easy matter, particularly now that the total looked more like a fellow Jain deserved. Thanks to this community spirit of a stranger, Ravi was placed fourth in the final list of merit scholars and he could settle down to study for a career without worrying about next month's tuition and residence fees.

Community spirit extends way beyond helping a stranger of the same sect. Acquaintances bombarded Nirmala with information about girls of marriageable age for Ravi's older brothers, all of them of "fair complexion, from good families, educated but modest and family-minded." When Nirmala told Santosh about a desirable proposal for him he was blunt, "You need to get your head examined. Do you expect me to support a wife and send you hundred rupees as well? Or you have come into some money I do not know of. If you need me to send you what I do now, you better tell them to wait till Ravi has started earning." But Satya had different ideas. He felt that a wife would help his career by enhancing social contacts with senior officers through their wives. He specified a girl who was outgoing, not one who was conventional and shy. Within a couple of months Nirmala received the proposal from a family of grain traders in Meerut. After Pundit Guru Ram pronounced the horoscopes compatible, a meeting of the two families was arranged and the intended couple met for the first time. Satya and Geeta, who was four years younger than him, talked privately for a few minutes and liked each other. That was enough preparation for a life time of intimate companionship. When asked what kind of dowry they would like Nirmala sent the message, "We may be short in worldly goods but we are not so poor in spirit as to demand a dowry. We are content with the Bahu that will add to our family's good name. Whatever you want to send with your daughter for her home is your decision. All we wish is a good reception for a small wedding party of about fifty people." Holy men from both families agreed on a date three months later when the stars were in harmony.

Along with the the wedding preparations, there was a dark cloud on the family horizon. Rishi continued to lose weight while growing taller. He had no energy for any physical exertion at all. Nirmala took him to Dr. Mitra at regular intervals. His advice on the last visit was frank, "The heart problem is getting worse. I have no solution for it. If you could take him to some heart specialist in Delhi, he may suggest some operation to help him. It will be expensive but that is all that can be done at this stage."

"How expensive?" Ganesh asked. Rishi was his favourite son.

"You are looking at ten thousand or more. That is only for the operation. Hospital stay and your expenses in Delhi are extra. Total will be more than twenty." Dr. Mitra's words were harsh but true. After the pronouncement of the doctor, Ganesh's prayers became more urgent. But Lord Hanuman was too busy with other devotees and Rishi's health continued to deteriorate. It also touched a raw nerve in Nirmala. No one needed to tell her that twenty thousand would be nothing to her if she were born a boy and inherited her grandfather's wealth or if she let Kanaka arrange her marriage to a man of some means. She always defended Ganesh if anything critical of him was uttered. But she didn't really know whether it was love or refusal to acknowledge her teenage blunder.

10

Nineteen sixty was the year when the country's economy was falling apart due to bureaucratic blunders and rampant corruption. Universities were turning out brilliant graduates with no jobs to go to. The government departments were crowded with all levels of employees with little to do. The factories could not import the machines they needed to produce and couldn't ship what they produced because roads and rails were choking with traffic.

The day Ravi finished his studies and started work was perhaps the happiest day in Nirmala's life. She credited her prayers for Ravi finding a satisfactory job locally. He could stay at home and his salary of four hundred rupees was the most money she had ever had on a regular basis. She could cook rice and chapatis with two vegetable curries, pay off accumulated debts little by little and buy medicines that were prescribed to reduce Rishi's pain. She hired a dhobi and a maid and stopped adding water to the milk. She started to sleep better and Sarla happily wrote to Kanaka that her niece was looking younger than her forty years.

Ravi's job involved a lot of travel. He was paid overtime and expenses and he quite enjoyed visiting various operations of the company. However, it bothered him that his senior colleagues stayed in better hotels and were allowed other privileges. The worst part was that he was better trained and often needed to tactfully direct them to the right course of action. He reviewed his options and an unexpected window opened up. Ravi looked up from the newspaper and said to Nirmala who was serving him the usual breakfast of paratha and hot milk, "An Indian branch of a British company is advertising for applications for all expenses paid post-graduate studies in U.K. Wonder whether I should get the application form." Hot paratha slipped out of Nirmala's grasp. There was an awkward silence till she said, "You are not going to leave me a destitute again. I will be lost without you. I am not going to let you go. I have made enough sacrifices, now I need some respite from the constant worry. Forget about the application forms. Save the stamp for writing to Amma. She is anxious to hear when you are going to see her."

Ganesh intervened with a life line, at least that is what it appeared to Ravi, "Let him send the application. If, Hanumanji willing, he wins it he can use it as a bargaining chip for promotion."

"All right, I will let you apply. But don't think you are going anywhere. Think of Rishi even if you don't think of us. This is final; you are applying to get a promotion here. I will pray for you, but not for you going away. Bhagwan will listen to me as He has in the past."

At nine on the morning of the interview there were eleven other candidates in the waiting room. They were all top students from major universities in India. Every one of them was dressed in a suit and a tie even though it was the height of summer. Ravi, on the other hand, was dressed in a light blue cotton T shirt and light corduroy pants. Each interview lasted half an hour and it was late in the afternoon when Ravi was called. He was less tired than bored. On his way to the interview room he sipped some water from the water fountain. It settled him somewhat. An orderly opened the door for him to enter. He raised his hands with palms together and bowed his head to greet the row of interviewers reclining on well padded chairs on the other side of a long mahogany table. He was directed to sit down on the empty chair facing them. After a few preliminary questions to make sure he was the right candidate, the interviewers got down to the job of testing the breadth of his knowledge. He was surprised when an interviewer questioned him in depth on the subject of his postgraduate thesis which Dr. Ghosh, his thesis supervisor had just published in an American journal with him as co-author. When his time was up, this interviewer thanked him, asked him to convey his compliments to Prof. Ghosh and wished him success in whatever course his career followed.

Two weeks later Ravi received a thick envelope informing him of the award and providing detailed information about all the things he needed to do to prepare for his time in UK. He put these aside and started to work out in his mind on how to tackle Mr. Negi, the superintendent with whom he needed to negotiate the promotion. He wrote a short letter requesting a meeting "to discuss my options in light of the scholarship I have been awarded." He received a short reply setting the meeting at 4:00 PM the following Thursday.

Mr. Negi's office was in a different building, a couple of miles from Ravi's office. He cycled there to arrive a few minutes early and was glad to see that there was no other visitor waiting in the reception room. The secretary informed the boss of Ravi's arrival and was told to ask him to wait. Ravi sat down on one of a row of steel chairs and picked a newspaper from the sidetable. There was not much of interest happening in the world and time passed slowly. After an hour the secretary picked up her bag and left telling him to stay. At long last Ravi heard the footsteps from the office. He looked at the clock, it showed seven o'clock. Footsteps came closer, Mr. Negi was coming out of his office and Ravi stood up to greet him. But Mr. Negi walked past him without the faintest acknowledgement and got into his car waiting at the entrance. Ravi cycled home utterly devastated. Nirmala and Ganesh were eagerly waiting for him. They looked at him and knew that something was wrong. "Did you see Mr. Negi?" they asked.

"He kept me waiting for three hours and went home without seeing me even though he knew I was in the reception room," Ravi replied rushing past them to hide his moist eyes.

Crestfallen does not begin to describe how his parents felt.

The non-interview caused turmoil in Ravi's head. The humiliation was followed by anger made worse by his helplessness. "I am angry for a good reason but I can not afford to be irrational. I have to stay in the job; the family needs the money I bring in. I can't imagine the circumstances which will allow me to accept the scholarship. Still, there is no harm in finding out what others have to say," he reasoned. He started sounding relatives for advice on what he should do. Nirmala was adamant that Ravi should not go, "You promised me" she repeated every time the issue came up. Ganesh was inclined in that direction too but not that sure. Rishi felt that his illness was a major factor in this decision and told Ravi that he should do what he was comfortable with. Most other relatives were divided more or less evenly. Then there was the issue of guarantee. To access the scholarship he had to find someone who would promise to repay the full scholarship amount if Ravi did not return to India. Shivanand was the only person he knew with means to do it but Ravi did not have the nerve to approach him.

The company instructed Ravi to go on a two week tour of a factory near Calcutta, his haunt during student days. He thought it was a godsend; it would allow him to consider all factors coolly. Travel was much more comfortable now than in his student days; the company paid for a second class sleeping birth. Standing in a crowded compartment for a day and a half had become a distant memory. He could order meals from the dining room and recline in comfort while sipping tea from a china cup. Pros and cons of accepting the scholarship were starting to form clearly in his mind. When he got off the train at his destination he felt confident that he would know what to do by the time his visit was over.

Nirmala and Ganesh were at the station to welcome him back when his train pulled up at the platform. Although it was the month of July, Ganesh was wearing a sweater and Nirmala was wrapped in a woolen shawl. "A cool morning?" he thought. He wanted to tell them his decision as soon as possible, "Rishi's illness makes it impossible for me to go. It is my duty to ensure his remaining days are comfortable. I will swallow the insult, turn the scholarship down and hope the promotion comes soon." But something in the demeanour of his parents stopped him from saying it. Ganesh hugged him, something he rarely did and tears rolled down from his eyes on to Ravi's shoulders, "Rishi fell ill soon after you left and passed away last Tuesday. He developed severe chest pain. Dr. Mitra said his heart was pushing hard against the walls. He lay silent with his eyes closed, his face distorted in pain. In spite of the unbearable pain your brother was thinking of the family and you. After suffering for two days he uttered his last words 'let Ravi Bhaiya go' and stopped breathing."

Ravi was shocked. This eventuality was the one that had never crossed his mind. Eyes moist, he hugged Nirmala and they silently followed the coolie to the rickshaw.

Nirmala made special parathas from ground lentil and stuffed with potatoes and spinach. After serving Ravi a couple with hot milk, she looked him in the eye and said, "It will be a bad omen to go against Rishi's last words. Start getting ready to leave. But you are going for two years and not a day more. I want you here as soon as the time is up. I will talk to Mausiji about your guarantee."

4

Trying Times

(1961–1971)

*D*uring the late nineteen sixties and seventies the crème de la crème of young Indian talent departed for the West, often paid by the government to do so. The loss of talent, not really needed in India at that time, had a payback in the dollars and pounds these expatriates sent home, especially since the country was desperately short of foreign currency. The high calbre of students also raised the prestige of Indian schools because their graduates distinguished themselves in many professions.

1

Six weeks after Rishi's death, Ravi left for England. Nirmala held back her tears but the dam broke the moment train was out of sight. She pushed Ganesh away when he tried to console her, "Stay away from me. You have no feelings and you never know how I feel. Losing two children as babies was bad but nothing like losing two grown up ones. With Ravi has gone the peace of mind I had for a few months. If fate has decreed misery, that is all I will have. All the sins of past lives continue to haunt me. I must have murdered someone's children for such relentless suffering in this life. I wish I were dead rather than Rishi. I could not even get him the operation he needed. Now Ravi has left me. I am sure he won't come back. He is as good as dead so far as I am concerned."

Ganesh interrupted her, "Don't say such things. You never know what reaches God's ears and is treated as your wish. We should pray for his prompt return and long life. Every thing will turn out for the best as it always does. Thanks to Hanumanji we still have two sons here. He will look after us all."

Nirmala went to bed and cried herself to sleep. Ganesh slumped on the floor in the courtyard under the twinkling stars in a clear sky, his hands folded and head bowed in prayer.

Ravi sent colourful cards from every port where the ship docked with no news other than "All is well."

"Nothing about food, about other passengers, sea sickness or anything. For all we know he has started to eat meat or has fallen for a white girl on the ship." At long last a thick envelope arrived with English stamps.

"It was a great voyage. Some passengers got sea sick but not me. It is because I stuck to vegetarian dishes and drank milk and water. No alcohol for me even though it was free. The University is even more impressive than the IIT. So many buildings and so much equipment in the labs! The main library has ten rooms, each room bigger than our house. You will be happy to know that Dr. Newsohm, my professor, sees no reason why I won't be finished in two years if I work hard. The Indian consul helped me find a room in a hostel with men and women from all over the world. I have made some friends, other Indian students. Some girls tried to talk to me but I did not know what to say to them. Now they leave me alone."

The news from Ravi was not the only happy event of the day. A letter from Geeta from Allahabad where Satya was posted conveyed the news that she had been waiting for three years, "I went to see the doctor to get a prescription for upset stomach because I had been throwing up. He checked me and gave the great news. We are expecting a baby at last. It is due in April. The doctor advised me to take it easy. My mother is not well and I can not go to Meerut. Will you be able to come and stay with us till the baby settles down and I am feeling well again?"

A week later Nirmala and Ganesh were in Allahabad. Geeta had not been able to digest the food and was feeling run down. Nirmala prepared lentil and tomato soups, puffed up chapatis to be eaten without butter and weak tea with just one spoon of sugar. Geeta could digest the simple unspiced dishes and started to regain her health. Nirmala's tender loving care got her back on her feet. She was in good spirits at the harvest festival of Dipawali. On the morning of the holy day Nirmala said to Satya, "We should celebrate Geeta's recovery. The best way to do it is to distributed provision to feed homeless families."

"That is a good idea and it will be a good omen for the baby too," Saty agreed

"How many families and how much," asked Geeta.

"Send ten pounds of flour, five pounds of lentils and a pound of sugar to each family. That should be plenty."

"There are some large families among the orderlies who will be glad to receive some help," Satya agreed.

"Add some candy for the children," Ganesh advised.

A telegram arrived from Aminabad; Kanaka was seriously ill. Nirmala and Ganesh took the train for Ashapur and from there Nirmala took the bus and was at her mother's bedside the next day. Dr. Chatterjee was very frank, "Ammaji has no illness that I can diagnose. The only thing I can think is that the constant anxiety about you and your family has gradually drained all the life juices out of her and now the pot is empty. She does not eat, refuses medicines, stays in her bed all day and prays to the almighty to take her away. She needs someone to look after her full time. You should take her to Ashapur. She can be examined by the specialists there. Who knows, being near you may raise her spirits and help her recover. I am a simple village doctor. There is not much I can do for her."

Nirmala had to ask, "You know Doctor sahib what she thinks of my husband. Living in the same house with him could add to her agitation. How can I help that?"

"I know the problem. You will have to keep them apart somehow. I must warn you. She won't survive another month in Aminabad."

By a stroke of good fortune, Shivanand was returning home from Delhi in his car and, as was his custom, dropped by to see his sister-in-law. When he saw her condition and was told of the plans, he invited them to ride with him. Ganesh was shocked to see his mother-in-law being carried by the driver of his uncle into the house. "Why are you staring like that? Go and get a bed ready," Nirmala scolded. Ganesh went back inside and quickly put a mattress, a sheet, a pillow and a blanket on a string cot. When Kanaka had been laid down Ganesh folded his hands in greeting. Kanaka stared at him for a moment or two then turned her head towards the wall.

Dr. Mitra examined Kanaka thoroughly and drew some blood for tests. "Dr. Chatterjee was right, there is nothing basically wrong. She is run down and I can't prescribe any medicine. What she needs is rest and some caring. Give her a small glass of hot milk several times a day and some tomato soup at meal times. Make sure she doesn't get excited. She needs to stay calm," he advised.

Nirmala knew what Dr. Mitra meant by excitement and advised Ganesh to stay out of Kanaka's sight. She attended to her mother's smallest need. Nirmala and Ganesh talked only when. Kanaka was asleep and even then in whispers. Non-prescriptions of two doctors worked and she improved steadily. Nirmala breathed a big sigh of relief when Kanaka got up by herself to use the toilet after a month. But Nirmala's caregiving duties were far from over.

Ganesh's illness started with a cold which everyone thought would go away after regulation three days. But it got worse and he started complaining of breathlessness. Dr. Mitra diagnosed pneumonia and prescribed some pills. Nirmala counted her money, it was barely enough for the necessities for the week before the money order from Santosh would arrive. All the caring for Geeta and Kanaka had sapped her own energy and the physical and mental exhaustion contributed to her fateful decision. She chose food over medicine.

———◇◇———

Ganesh's condition deteriorated but he had guessed Nirmala's predicament and did not raise any fuss. However, his mind could not fool the body. Nirmala woke up with an eerie feeling on Monday morning. She went to Kanaka's bed and was relieved to see her breathing normally. But when she saw Ganesh she let out a scream. His face was pale and his body still. She felt his wrist, it was cold. She put her palm on his chest; she did not feel the heart beat. Dr. Mitra came over straight away and confirmed her suspicion. "I did not get the medicine because there was no money left after buying food," tearful Nirmala told him on his way out.

"Don't blame yourself," Dr. Mitra said. His condition was much too serious for medicines to have worked for long. It was God's will. You can't fight that." Nirmala believed him; her conscience needed the balm.

Nirmala and Kanaka settled down to the life of two widows, one who had lost everything with her husband's death so many years ago and the other who had nothing left to lose when her husband passed away. In some respects Nirmala's life was easier than it had been lately; she had only one person to take care of, she did not have the fear of Kanaka's unpleasantness to her husband, and it was a little easier to manage with the money she received from her sons. Ravi's regular letters were consoling. His work was going well and he fully expected to return in two years. Satya had been promoted to a higher rank, Geeta was in good spirits with baby due anytime now and Santosh was winning acclaim for his essays on the benefits of simple living.

Another year went by. Geeta and Satya visited for a week with their boy Beeju who reminded Nirmala and Kanaka of Ravi when he was a baby. The horoscope predicted a great future for him too. Nirmala told every one that the baby would grow up to be an engineer and go to Vilayat—abroad—to study. Santosh thought it was time for him to get married but Nirmala was dithering about seeking proposals; it did not seem appropriate so soon after the deaths of his brother and his father.

2

It had been fifteen months since Ravi's departure. The heat of summer was doused by the recent rains and the cold of winter had not yet set in. The letters, short and somewhat monotonous arrived regularly every two weeks from England. Then the postman delivered a thick envelope with stamps bearing the Queen's image in many colours. Nirmala's hand shook with excitement as she signed the receipt and gave the elderly man a rupee before tearing it open. Along with the usual one page letter there were six photographs, two of them of a young white girl with beautiful eyes, pretty face and short dark hair. The other four were of Ravi and the girl in various poses in a beautiful garden with strange trees and flowers. The girl appeared younger but towered over him. The actual colour of her eyes and hair was impossible to judge from the black and white photographs. The letter said she was a friend called Monica who lived in the same hostel. Kanaka did not believe this "friend talk"She asked Nirmala, "Why would he send her picture if not to prepare us for the bad news?"

"He promised me he would be back in two years," Nirmala shot back. After a long pause, she added, "He has always kept his word with me. Vilayat can change him but not so much that he will let his mother down. Mark my words; he will be here in six months. And alone, not with a Gori mem sahib."

Kanaka was not to be silenced so easily, "He is a great catch for any one, whether one of ours or a Gori. Look at the way they look at each other. The writing is clear on the wall. The fish is in the net. You are not going to see him in six months or in six years. I will go on the pyre without seeing him." She wiped her eyes with her white cotton sari. Nirmala turned away silently and went to the verandah clutching the letter and the pictures. She did not want Ammaji to see her own tears.

As always, Nirmala wrote her reply the same evening. "Beta, khush raho. Amma and I are happy that you are meeting nice people and making friends with locals in a strange country. Monica seems like a good person to have as a friend. Send us the pictures of your other friends in your next letter."

Kanaka meant what she said about the pictures and her heart did not take kindly to it. She had pain in her chest and she could not keep any food down. Dr. Mitra prescribed medicines to reduce pain but she refused to take them. Nirmala asked Sarla to talk some sense in her sister. When Sarla failed, Panditji was called in but Kanaka stuck to her guns. No one knows whether it was starvation or heart attack, barely a month had gone by after viewing the photos of Ravi and Monica, when Nirmala heard her mother's last words, "Hare Ram, I am coming."

Her mother's death coming so soon after the deaths of her son and her husband caused Nirmala immense grief. The thought that had plagued her all her life went around her mind like a spinning wheel, "The sins of my past lives are responsible for all my misfortunes in this life." Then a new idea cropped up, "The only way to wash off these sins is to give up the temptations of normal life and become a sanyasin." She decided this is what she must do.

———◇◇———

Santosh took the ashes of Kanaka to Haridwar after thirteen days of lament to deposit them in the holy Ganges. Nirmala was sitting cross legged on a mat, looking forlorn, when Satya returned after seeing his brother off at the bus station. He took his chappals off, sat down next to her. Next to the imposing figure of her Air Force officer son, shriveled figure of Nirmala looked even tinier. Satya put his hand on his mother's. Feel of the leathery skin and brittle bones added to his distress and he needed some moments to compose himself. Finally he said, "Maaji, I want you to come with us to Bangalore. Geeta will look after you and Beeju needs a grandma."

"It is nice of you to ask me to live with you. But I can't do it."

"Why not? What is stopping you?"

"I have caused misfortune after misfortune ever since I was born. First it was my father, now Rishi, your Pitaji and Ammaji. All these misfortunes are due to the sins in my former life and sins in this life have made the burden heavier. I am going to wash these off in this life if Bhagwan gives me enough time."

"Even if it were true, how would you achieve that?"

"I have thought it over. I am becoming a sanyasin. A group of pilgrims is visiting our temple next month. I am going to settle all my affairs by then and join them. Don't waste your energy in telling me otherwise. My mind is made up."

"Maaji, you can't go walking around in summer. It will kill you. Spend the summer with us and think about it some more. If you still want to go on the pilgrimage when it has cooled off after the monsoon we can discuss the best way to do it. Geeta is so looking forward to caring for you and getting you back into good health."

"No, Satya. You may not agree, but I know what I want to do and I will do it. Go and see Geeta in the kitchen. She needs your help."

———◊◊———

Nirmala gave away all her possessions and joined the band of pilgrims on a tour of holy places in India. Satya and Santosh waited for a while for her, but when she did not return they put their trust in Lord Mahavir and got on with their lives. Nirmala lived austerely, traveling all over the country by train, bus, cart and in bare feet on cold dirt and hot tarmac. She spent nights under a pipal tree and if she was lucky in a Dharmshala attached to the temple she was visiting, eating whatever the donors were handing out and praying for the forgiveness of her sins and the welfare of her sons, including the one who chose to neglect his promise to her for a Gori.

3

Jawahar Lal Nehru died in 1964 and after two other short term leaders, his daughter Indira Gandhi became the Prime Minister in 1966. In between there was another war with Pakistan. Indira Gandhi continued the socialist policies of her father and the economy of the country stayed in the doldrums. The social upheaval in the West had only a marginal impact on India.

Years of abstemious living and constant travelling took their toll on Nirmala. She lost more weight and started to cough. One day she was resting on a tattered cotton sheet on the ground, staring at a mynah bird singing on a branch above her when a young woman sat down near her ragged feet and started massaging them with her bare hands. Not only did this comfort her feet, her whole body felt relaxed. After enjoying the feeling for a while she said "Ah, it feels so good. Child, what is your name and what are you doing here?

"Maaji, I am Veeshu. My poor widowed mother married me off to an old man with six grown children. Soon after the wedding he passed away. My step children drove me from the house and I decided to spend my life in the service of Bhag-wanji. Maaji, would you like to tell me what made you leave the world behind?"

"Dear Veeshu, I am so sorry to hear of your grief. I too had my misfortunes, so many and so quickly that I too decided to devote the rest of my life in search of the true path to Bhagwan."

"Maaji, I have noticed that you do not like talking to other people. Do you mind telling me some of your tragedies?"

"Where do I begin? My youngest son died, the apple of my eye left for Vilayat and was snared by a Gori, then my husband and mother died, all within two years. I could not face living with my other sons, just in case I brought them some misfortune too. I have been on the pilgrimage since my mother left us."

"Maaji, I am sorry to hear of your distress. Will you mind this girl younger than your sons telling you something?" Vee-shu asked still massaging the feet.

"Of course, not. What do you have to tell me?"

"Just this, Maaji. You are not strong enough for the life of a sanyasin now. You should consider returning to your sons."

"I do have good sons but why will they want this old woman around the house?"

"Because you are their mother, Maaji. You could help them with your wisdom and your grandchildren need you too."

"What if I bring them misfortune?"

"Maaji, every person has his own fortune. You do not impose your fortune on them. Whatever is written on their palm will be their fate. You being with them or away from them matters less than the tiniest spec of dust."

"Aah! it hurts all over," groaned Nirmala. Then the baby face of Satya's son Beeju and the thought of the regard Geeta always had for her crossed her mind. "Maybe it is worth a try. How do I find out where Satya is though?" she whispered, more to herself than to Veeshu.

"Maaji, leave it to me."

5

Reconciliation

(1971–1972)

he nineteen seventies were hard times in India. The overwhelming victory over Pakistan and the creation of Bangladesh in 1971 made the Indians euphoric, even those who were opposed to the autocratic Prime Minister Indira Gandhi. It made her more determined to follow her rigid policies even though the economy continued to deteriorate. The protest movements started again after a short respite. Iron-fisted Indira and her son Sanjay imposed harsh regulations. Protest movements, some peaceful and a few violent, started all over the country. The self-righteous dictatorial daughter of Jawahar Lal Nehru, a champion of democratic rule till his dying day, did not relent and prisons were filled with protesters.

1

When the war in Bangla Desh appeared on horizon, Air Force transferred Satya to Delhi to improve communication with various centres and moved his family to the outskirts of the metropolis within easy distance of his office. It was mid morning, the sun was not yet at its peak and the heat was still tolerable. Geeta saw an old woman stumbling on the gravel path towards the front door. She was small, emaciated, dressed in rags and leaning on a stick for support as she hobbled, "Beeju, there is an old woman coming to the door, give her this," Geeta said picking a coin from the dish. Then she looked at the woman more closely and the coin dropped from her hand. The woman was her mother-in-law. Her heart jumped to the ceiling with joy and she rushed to touch Nirmala's feet. She called Mohan, a sixteen year old boy who helped her with the chores, and they carried Nirmala to a bed in the shady part of the courtyard. They arranged the pillows so Nirmala could recline comfortably and covered her legs with a light blanket. Geeta asked Mohan to make Halwa and tea and phoned Satya, "I have great news!,How quickly can you come home?"

"What news? Can't it wait?" Satya barked in his usual tense telephone voice.

"Maaji is here."

"I will be home in ten minutes." Satya put the phone down, issued instructions to his secretary and rushed to greet his mother. He saw Beeju, now almost eight years old, shyly watching the proceedings from a distance. Satya picked him up and placed him next to Maaji. He noticed straight away that not much was well with the condition of his mother and he went to the telephone and set up an appointment for a thorough check-up with the chief medical officer in the military hospital the next day.

Nirmala described all the temples she visited and how much joy she received from each prayer without mentioning the hardships, coughing fits and the debilitating of last few weeks. Satya told her his exploits in the war—how he kept the Air Force supplied. Geeta told her all the news of family and friends. Sarla had arranged for Santosh to marry a girl much younger than him and the couple was very happy. Geeta brought the wedding picture from the mantelpiece and handed it to Maaji.

"She looks plain and short but appearances don't matter as long as she makes him happy," Nirmala remarked feeling remorse at not having any role in selecting the bride and arranging the wedding.

There was other news. Many relatives had various ailments and a few were in excellent health. There were marriages and new births but fortunately no deaths. Then came the most important news from Geeta, "Maaji, I am expecting our second baby in six months."

"That is great news. I hope I am not too much bother. You need rest and looking after, not an invalid around you."

"Maaji, you should not worry, least of all about me. You will be fine long before I need help. Everyone has been so worried about you. Ravi has been sending worried letters about absence of letters from you. There is a stack of letters from him and some from elsewhere waiting for you. They will wait till you have eaten and have had some rest. A few more hours in my drawer will not make any difference to them or us," Geeta said and Satya nodded agreement.

2

Nirmala woke up with a start. The clock on the wall said 7:25 and it was bright outside. Geeta came in with a tumbler of tea, "Maaji, you were sleeping so soundly we thought you needed sleep more than food. You sip this tea and I will bring parathas and Halwah in a minute. You have slept for eighteen hours; You must be starving."

"I am hungry but not starving. I must have my bath and prayer before I can eat. Can the food wait half an hour?"

"Of course the food will wait. I will get hot water ready for your bath. Come down to the bathroom after your tea. I will help you. I will get clothes out of your bag too."

After the short version of prayer followed by a hearty breakfast, Nirmala sat cross-legged on the bed with packets of letters in front of her. She arranged them in order of importance to her, least important first and most important, from Ravi, last. She read each letter slowly, putting the ones that needed response in a neat pile on her left, and the others in a heap on her right. It was nearly eleven when she was ready to cut the string around the last packet. Just as Mohan handed her the scissors, Satya came in to take her for the medical appointment.

The CMO greeted Nirmala like his own mother. He bent down to touch her feet but she moved away, "No, you don't touch my feet. I am a humble poor woman and you are a famous doctor."

"Namaste, Maaji. You are a sanyasin. Every one knows the story of your life of sacrifice and your pilgrimage. I am blessed Satyaji has brought you to my clinic and not taken you to a bigwig in private practice. If you do not mind sitting on this chair we will get down to business."

He was very methodical and did not say a word except to ask "Does it hurt?" as he pressed against her body at critical points. When he was finished he turned to Satya and said in Hindi so Nirmala could understand, "Maaji is very weak and needs a lot of care. She does not have to stay in bed but should not exert physically any more than absolutely necessary. Her organs are fine except that I want to get an X-Ray of her chest and some other tests I will write down for you. She needs some iron but I don't think she can absorb it just yet. Give her as much tomato shorba, milk and lentils as she will have. She needs some looking after but there is nothing to worry about. Not till I get the test results."

After a light lunch of chapati and lentils Nirmala resumed her cross-legged sitting position on the bed with her mail. Ravi's letters were the same as those she remembered—short, with nothing about what he did all day other than work. Some of them had cheques of varying amounts. "I have found a job paying more in a month than I would earn in India in a year." "I am traveling all over Europe and America and preparing myself for a big position in India." Then the shock: a long letter with several pictures requesting her permission to marry Monica. The pictures were of the two of them, both looking older than she remembered from the first set of eight years ago, happy as larks with arms around each other, she towering over him with her brown hair cut above the neck and her skirt barely reaching the knees.

Nirmala broke into sobs lamenting over and over "Amma was right. Now he will never come back. Oh Bhagwan! What sins did I commit in my last life? What more do I have to suffer?" Geeta rushed in, sat by her holding her in a tight embrace. She had sense to wait till Nirmala had calmed down somewhat before asking what had caused the upset.

"Look, here is the letter. He wants to marry that giant of a Gori with bare legs and short hair. I lost my husband, my mother, my son. Now I am losing another son. I must have killed a million innocent children in my former life to deserve this punishment."

Geeta looked at the picture of the smiling young girl with a pleasant face and tried to console her mother-in-law, "Maaji, she has to wear what every one else wears. She appears to me to be a really nice young woman. Bhaiya would not fall for some ordinary person, would he?"

"Ordinary or not, it doesn't matter. Now he will not come back. We have lost him. My Ravi has been stolen from me. You will never see your devar again. He was to look after me in my old age. Now I will be a burden on you and Santosh."

"Maaji, you are making a big tale out of a little letter. If you don't want him to marry, don't give your permission. Even better, tell him that he can marry only if he comes back to live here. And why do you talk of burden. You will never be a burden on anyone. Every person I know worships the ground you walk on. You are doing us a great favour by living with us. I can use your advice in managing the family."

"I have to reconcile myself to another loss. This is my fate. Bhagwan give me strength to suffer this just as you have helped me through all else."

"Maaji, your son will be home soon. Let him think over the problem, he is very good at resolving such issues. I must go and look after the tea. You look at that photo again. She is a nice girl and will make a good partner for Bhaiya."

Geeta called Satya with a summary of events. On his return he went straight to his mother who was not sobbing now but still staring at a picture. He asked with a smile, "Maaji, who are you looking at so intently?"

"I am looking at my new daughter-in-law. Your brother decided we could not find him a wife, so he found one himself. She seems all right, as much as one can tell from a photo. But he will not come back," and Nirmala burst into tears again.

Satya put his arms around her body and it struck him again how thin his mother had become. He held her hand with his other hand and said in a calm voice, "Maaji, listen to an Air Force officer. These days you can travel faster from the farthest corner of the world by air than from Calcutta to Delhi by train. It costs a little more but what does it matter if he is earning a lot. Here is a suggestion. Why don't you ask them to come here for their honeymoon? They can see whether India will suit her and we can see whether the new member of the family is a worthy addition."

Nirmala was not consoled but she agreed to follow her son's advice. Satya helped Nirmala draft the invitation and it was posted to catch the first mail collection next morning.

3

Sunday was hectic for every one in the household in preparation for the arrival of Ravi and his bride early next morning. A "WELCOME HOME" banner in English and Hindi was hung at the entrance; red, green and blue balloons were suspended from hooks and invitations were sent out to all relatives for a reception on Thursday evening. A western toilet was installed and twelve rolls of toilet paper were placed in a basket next to it. The old fashioned string bed in the guest room was replaced by a rented modern double mattress bed with a canopy of mosquito net. Geeta made preparations for breakfast so that it would be ready soon after the hungry travelers arrived. Satya bought Ravi's favourite sweets, ras malai and sandesh and two packets of digestive biscuits for Monica. They went to bed early because Geeta and Satya planned to leave an hour before the arrival of the flight due at five in the morning. Nirmala slept fitfully, praying for the safe flight every time her sleep was interrupted.

The flight was late as usual. Satya was irritated and complained that Geeta had made him come early. Geeta was not in the mood to be told off, "If we were late, the flight would be early. And how do you know when they will close a road for some VIP or there is a traffic jam. Let us sit in the café and have a cup of chai with samosas. That will make the time pass." Satya was happy that the idea had come from his wife. He felt that if he had suggested it she would have called it a waste of money.

No sooner had the waiter brought their order, than the arrival of Pan AM flight from London was announced. Satya got up to leave.

"What is the rush?" Geeta, practical as always, said. "It will take some time to clear customs and immigration. We can have our tea and watch from here for the passengers. There couldn't be that many brown and white young couples on the plane."

Satya sat down again, added two spoonfuls of sugar to his tea, poured mint chutney on a samosa, looked at his watch and said with the authority of an Indian husband, "You are right, we have at least ten minutes to enjoy the snack. It is costing us plenty."

He was wrong again. It was an hour before they saw the couple, a thin, tall white young woman, much younger than they had imagined, dressed in a purple sari with a broad brocade border and a short rather chubby slightly balding on top man, looking older than they expected, dressed in a khaki shirt and blue pants, each pulling a large suitcase. Satya shouted 'Ravi' and rushed towards them. Ravi stood a little behind Monica as she bent down to touch Satya's feet. She did the same when Geeta caught up with them. The brothers hugged each other as Geeta pulled Monica up and hugged her. "The brothers could be twins, same height, same face," Monica said to Geeta.

———◇◇———

It was after seven and bright daylight when the car stopped in front of the house. Nirmala was waiting in the porch with a welcoming smile. Satya opened the door for Monica who got out of the small car rather clumsily not being used to the folds of the sari. Nirmala noticed that she towered above every one else but was shy and gentle in manner and not in the least domineering. Whether it was the sari dragging on the ground or the chappals or the uneven ground, Monica walked slowly towards Nirmala, bent down and touched her bare feet. Nirmala did not expect such modesty from a Gori and said, "Array, kya kar rahi ho? Utho, main to mooh dekhna chahti hun." Monica guessed that it meant "Hey, what are you doing, stand up, I want to see your face" and stood up folding her hands, her body bent so her head was just a little higher than that of her mother-in-law. Nirmala patted her on the head and on the back and led every one in. It was only then she noticed Ravi who was smiling to himself happy with the reception Monica had received. He touched Nirmala's feet before expressing his consternation, "Maaji, you look very thin. What have you been doing to yourself? "

Satya interrupted, "That is a long story I will tell you later. Go, brush your teeth and shave and make Monica comfortable in the room to your right. There is a bucket of hot water in the bathroom. Your Bhabhi will have the breakfast ready in ten minutes."

Monica asked Geeta, "Bhabhiji, what can I do to help?"

Geeta replied with a smile, "Go wash your face. You will have plenty of opportunity to help later. Maaji needs help with her bath. You can help her when she is ready."

Nirmala sat in a chair nearby while the family was having the breakfast. She did not eat before her prayers and she could not pray till she had a cleansing bath. Mohan served parathas at regular intervals to go with pea and potato curry, yoghurt, halvah and chai. They all talked, often at the same time, some sentences in English, some in Hindi, every word translated for the benefit of Monica and Nirmala. Conversation drifted from old times in Ashapur to the time they had been apart, to the bereavements and Nirmala's pilgrimage. Monica expressed her sympathy and admiration for the courage that Nirmala displayed in undertaking the pilgrimage. Satya gave a detailed account of her current health and what was being done. Nirmala and Monica participated in the conversation and their faces had broad smiles when looking at each other.

Santosh, his wife Kashi and their two boys arrived when the family was still at the table. Santosh was a slightly older replica of his brothers except that his kurta and pajama were made of khaddar popularized by Mahatma Gandhi during the independence movement. Kashi, short, plump and of kindly mien, was dressed in a cotton sari and had a prominent red dot on her forehead just above her nose. Monica got up when Satya introduced them to her and touched their feet, first Santosh's and then Kashi's. Kashi blessed Monica, "Khush raho" and hugged her new sister-in-law fondly. Monica patted children on their heads, asked their names and ages and told them they looked fabulous. Beeju brought toys to play with the boys. Mohan pulled up the chairs for Santosh and Kashi and served them chai. Geeta insisted that they had some parathas. She duly resisted till Mohan placed the thalis in front of them anyway.

Nirmala asked Mohan for hot water before he started to clear the table. Monica asked her, "Maaji, Bhabhiji asked me to help you with the bath. Will you let me do that?"

"Aray dekho, Gori bahu nahane main madad karegi, jaroor, jaroor," Nirmala replied and Satya translated, "Hey look, white daughter-in-law will help with the bath, sure sure."

Monica joined Nirmala in the bathroom. The Indian bath was a new experience for her. There were two buckets of water on the concrete floor, one hot and one cold, in front of a stool three inches high. A small jug, various soaps and shampoo were in an alcove in the brick wall. She helped Nirmala undress and sit on the stool. She noticed how difficult it was for Nirmala to manipulate her body which was even more emaciated than her face indicated. Her dark brown skin felt rough and it looked so tender as if it would split on slightest touch. Her hair was grey and thin, several teeth were missing.

Monica mixed some hot and some cold water in the jug, felt it with her index finger and poured it over Nirmala's head. Then she soaped her body and shampooed her hair. Nirmala then directed Monica to pour more water over her head and shoulders when she rubbed herself to get shampoo and soap off. When the water was used up Monica helped her mother-in-law to stand up and dried her body. She brought a set of clean clothes—petticoat, sari and blouse—from an alcove and helped her dress. Nirmala said some words in Hindi which Monica understood to be an expression of pleasure and gratitude. Monica nodded and said bravely in her broken Hindi "I am very happy" Nirmala looked even happier and then pointed to the door. Monica took the hint and left Nirmala to pray.

When Monica joined the rest of the group she could feel the goodwill from every corner. Her new relations had been singing her praises. She found Geeta in the kitchen and asked, "Bhabiji, can I help with the dishes?" Geeta disappointed her again, "Durga, the maid, comes in around this time to look after dishes and wash and iron the clothes. Usually she comes for a couple of hours every day but she has agreed to stay for the whole day when you are here. If you have any laundry put it in the basket in the room." Leaving the family to freely discuss their affairs in their mother tongue, Monica found Nirmala and joined her in prayer. Although she did not understand a word that was uttered, the recitations gave her a sense of tranquility.

While Nirmala was having her breakfast of paratha and lentil curry and a glass of lukewarm milk, Monica and Ravi disappeared into their room. A few minutes later they appeared loaded with packages of all sizes and shapes. Big boxes were handed to Geeta and Kashi, one soft roll to Satya, a small packet to Santosh, flat square boxes to Beeju and his cousins and a soft package was placed near Nirmala's feet by Monica. The boxes were accepted and put aside without a word but with expressions of delight. Ravi had to coax them to open their presents: blenders for sisters-in-law, leggo, books and paints for the boys, woolen cloth for a suit for Satya, a watch for Santosh. They were thrilled and said so. Monica was happy to see their delight but also a little surprised that no one actually said, "Thank you" to either of them. She mentioned it to Ravi when they were alone. His reply was what she expected, "Gratitude is felt, not expressed in words in our family. Don't expect any one of us to say 'Thank you' but you can be sure that favours are remembered and reciprocated whenever possible."

Nirmala was the last person to open her package. Ravi handed it to her, she shook it, felt it and said, "It is material for a dress that Monica will sew for me." Every one laughed, even more when Monica responded, "Maaji, I will make it for you if you will wear it." Beeju could not wait and tore the wrapping to reveal a thick tartan blanket. While Nirmala felt the soft weave Ravi said with some feeling, "Maaji, the men and women of Monica's clan wear skirts of this square design in these colours. She is sharing her family with you in return for you sharing your son with her."

"I can now feel close to her and through her to you when I wrap this around me as a shawl or as a blanket in bed." Both, Monica and Ravi noticed a tinge of melancholy in Nirmala's reply.

4

The home of Satya and Geeta was busier than the notorious traffic circle of Connaught Place in Delhi. There were hundreds of uncles and aunts, cousins called Jiji or Bhaiya, friends of Satya and Santosh and relatives of their wives who came to see their English relative. Monica could never have imagined so many people wanting to see her. Visitors brought bags of sweet and spicy delicacies which were consumed by those who followed. Mohan kept chai, lassi and cold water flowing. Geeta managed the guests with amazing skill and Monica wondered if such events were regular occurrences. Geeta explained the relationship to a lady who was approaching Monica with folded hands, "She is the wife of Deepu who is grandson of the sister of Kashi's grandfather."

"Sorry, I won't be able to remember such complex who is who when they return for the reception," Monica said. She added turning to Ravi "You will help me, won't you?"

"I will whenever I can." Ravi said. "I too have just met most of them for the first time."

On the morning of the party, during a welcome lull in the preparation, Nirmala, Ravi and Monica were by themselves in the courtyard at the back of the house enjoying the sun. Monica was speaking in broken Hindi and asking Nirmala about her recent life experiences. Nirmala was answering slowly so Monica could understand, and Ravi was helping when necessary. On a whim, without having discussed it with Ravi, Monica asked, "Maaji, I would love to go on a small pilgrimage with you to your favourite places. Next week will perhaps be the only time we could do it. What places do you suggest?"

Nirmala could not hide her surprise and asked Ravi, "Is Bahu really asking me to go to holy places with her?"

"Well, that is what she suggested," Ravi confirmed.

Nirmala paused for a long moment to recover, then replied "My favourite places within reasonable distance are Brindavan, the birth place of Lord Krishna and Jain temples of Dilwara. We can take in Taj Mahal in Agra and palaces in Jaipur with only a little diversion. We will need a good car with a reliable driver. It can be done on buses and trains but they are always late and you don't really have time to wait for them."

Satya almost hit his head on the ceiling when they told him of the plan a little later. "Maaji, you have not seriously considered the idea. First, you have not regained your health for this kind of travel. Second, it is not safe for any one, particularly a young foreign woman and her elderly mother-in-law to travel by themselves in that part of the country. I can't trust a driver, any driver, to look after you."

"Yes, that would be a problem," Geeta agreed.

"This comes as a shock to me. Ravi, did you have any inkling of this plan?" Satya asked.

"It was news to me too. But I understand Monica's wish to do something with Maaji which will please them both. I want to spend time with Maaji too. So I will go with them. Let us rent a car for a week. I know these places. I can be the chauffeur. I may not open the doors smartly but I am safe behind the wheel." Ravi replied.

"Geeta," Satya threw his hands up, turned to his wife and commanded, "remind me to talk to Ramesh chacha this evening about the car. Surendra mama will have leads to good guides. He wll find one to accompany our pilgrims." The man of the house had, as usual in an Indian home, the final word.

5

There was a gentle knock on the door. "It better be the cook," Geeta said moving towards the front door. Indeed it was the cook, a middle-aged skinny man with graying hair, dressed only in a loin cloth and standing in bare feet a couple of steps from the door with his head bowed. Geeta expressed her annoyance, "You are an hour late. How will you have all the sweets, samosas and pakoris made in time and not be late for Puris? You know that some guests arrive early and some don't eat after dark, don't you?"

"Mem sahib, don't be angry. You know me. Every thing will be ready on time as it always is."

"Don't flatter me with this Mem sahib business. Mem sahib is sitting there," Geeta said pointing to Monica. "Last time I had to cook myself for early diners. I don't want to do that today. I have enough to do as it is. You understand, don't you?"

"Ji Han, Mem sahib, I understand. Leave it all to me. Last time the sun set early. It will be fine today. I also have my son with me so I won't need Mohan to help me."

Geeta noticed his son standing at some distance with a big jute bag of utensils and other accoutrements of his trade balanced precariously on his head. This mollified her and she led them to the far end of the courtyard. Before long, the crackling of wood fire was replacing the hum from traffic.

Satya and Ravi got busy rearranging the furniture in every room. Monica was deputized to put away into cupboards and metal trunks whatever was not ornamental. Carpet rolls were pulled out from under beds and unrolled. Monica was handed cushions to puff up and place along the walls for people to sit on. Ravi pointed to some dead bulbs and helped Satya replace them. They tested the record player and picked the music. Satya asked Monica, "What do you prefer, pop or classical? We have some ghazals too. You know ghazals—love poems in Urdu which is not all that different from Hindi really."

"They are all Greek to me; choose whatever most people will like," Monica replied.

"Most people like pop. I know Ravi prefers Mom."

"Not funny," said Ravi and added, "I don't care what it is so long as it is not loud."

Monica offered to play a few records and set the volume. After a few songs she remarked, "It is great music. I don't know why Ravi hates Hindi films and pop music so much. We should go to a Hindi film before we leave."

"Take any record you want with you," Geeta offered generously and added "We can go to a movie tomorrow. It will help us recover from the party."

"Great idea. Let us go to the afternoon show at Odeon. Monica will like to see Sabka Gulam, the heart throb of Indian women," Satya said in support.

"Do we have to?" groaned Ravi.

"You don't have to. Look after Beeju and have a chat with Maaji." once again Satya had the final word.

Although the invitation was for six, guests started arriving at four. "We couldn't wait to see our Gori relative. Wouldn't be able to talk to her when the crowd is here," was the excuse. A throng arrived at five and the house was chock-a-block with people by six.

The guests came through the open door and walked straight to Nirmala, siiting on a chair, or Monica, standing a few feet away, whichever had a smaller gathering around her. The younger men and women tried to touch the feet of 'Maaji' even though she protested. Older guests greeted by smiling with hands folded in front of them and a slight bow. Then followed the concerned queries about her health; gratitude was expressed to their personal deity for her rapid recovery. She was congratulated by many for the addition to the family, but a few knew of her earlier reservations and did not mention it. The process was reversed with Monica. When older guests approached she bent down to touch their feet, they stopped her and greetings with folded hands were exchanged. With the frankness of their culture, every one closely examined Monica from head covered with the end of her red sari to toes peeping out of chappals and complimented her on her pleasant appearance, on the way sari suited her tall figure, her eyes, her hair, even her unpainted toes. There was no shortage of excited translators, some even repeated in the same language what they intended to translate into the other. Monica remembered either the face or the name of guests who had also visited earlier, never both, but they did not mind. Many older women relatives, keen to preserve the Hindu traditions, asked Ravi anxiously, "Do you eat meat now?" Ravi answered without batting an eyelid, "Of course not" so as not to hurt their feelings and added under his breathe, "when in India" to protect his integrity.

After greeting the host family, guests generally separated by gender and stood around in bunches, women chatting about their children's achievements and their own or their parent's illness, men about their businesses and national politics. When they felt peckish, they grabbed a metal plate, loaded it with their favourites from various dishes from a table along the wall and found a place to sit down on a chair or on a cushion on the carpet. Mohan and Durga filled the cups of chai for people having dinner. Monica was amazed that there was no bumping or pushing, people sensed when to shift a few inches to create a space and moved instinctively through the spaces only they could see.

Guests began to leave after dinner but not without a final chat with Monica and Nirmala. Ravi saw some older faces murmuring to Nirmala and guessed from their gestures that Monica had been approved by those who matter to the family. A flood of dinner invitations proved that the new addition was a hit with their generation too. The disappointment of an apologetic refusal was mitigated by the reason: they felt flattered that the Gori Bahu had proposed a pilgrimage with her mother-in-law.

6

During the confab at the party Ramesh Chacha offered to rent a car at the special family rate and suggested that the best use of time would be to fly back from Udaipur rather than spend two days in the car. He would send a driver to Udaipur to pick up the car and the guide. The time they save would be better spent in going to Ashapur to pay a visit to their Nanaji and Naniji, Shivanand and Sarla, who were in poor health.

"Oh, Ravi, let us do that. I do want to see the places you grew up in and meet the kind people who did so much for you when you were growing up," Monica interjected.

"You can take my car, I can do without for a couple of days," Satya suggested.

"Maaji should come too. She would like to see her Mausi-ji, I am sure," Monica contributed.

"She will be tired after the long trip and will need a rest after it. I do not think CMO will approve of two long journeys." Satya threw cold water on this idea.

Nirmala had the final word on this subject by saying, "I don't want to go to Ashapur for such a rushed trip. I have so many people to see there. I will go for a month when I am feeling better."

Ravi was diplomatic, "Chachaji, you are absolutely right. I should pay homage to the family patriarch and my benefactress and show Monica my childhood haunts. Are you sure you can spare the car, Bhaiya?"

"Oh yes, of course. I will have the Force driver pick me up. Don't you worry about the car and other little things," Satya said. He still patronized his younger brother.

Surendra Mama supported the travel plans and promised to arrange a guide for the tour. Satya booked three seats on a late evening flight from Udaipur to Delhi the following Sunday for their return trip.

On Sunday evening, an assistant of Ramesh Chacha brought the car; a late model Hindustan similar to the Morris Minor popular in the U.K. at that time. It was black; its leather bench seats in the front and back were covered with red velvety cloth to soothe vegetarian sensitivities. Ravi drove around the block to become familiar with it. When Mohan answered the gentle knock on the front door the next morning a stranger was standing in the porch with a small bundle.

"What do you want?" Mohan asked him rather rudely to show that he was someone important.

"Is this the home of Afsar Jain sahib?" the stranger asked disregarding the offensive tone.

"Yes it is. Who do you want to see?"

"I am Arvind, the guide. Surendra sahib asked me to be here at six sharp."

"They are still sleeping. It will be a while before they leave. Sit down on the bench. I will tell the sahib you are here when I return with the milk." Mohan directed the visitor to the steel furniture and rushed off to wait for the milkman and his cow.

Geeta was up early as usual and prepared the morning tea to serve others as they woke up. Things moved at leisurely pace and it was nearly ten when the luggage was brought to the car. Ravi and Monica watched Satya with amazement as he supervised the loading in a rather small trunk of two cases of clothing, a large bag of towels and two rolls of bedding which Geeta insisted they must carry. Nirmala was made comfortable on the passenger side of the back seat with a couple of cushions and a blanket. The lunch basket was placed in between her and Monica on the seat and the bag of precious toilet rolls on the floor. Arvind was in the front passenger seat to direct Ravi. He was a small man with a rather shrill voice. His boyish face belied his thirty years, a wife and two children. His general countenance was that of a proud man whom you take lightly at your peril. He was born and brought up in a village where they spoke a different dialect and Ravi had some difficulty with his accent. When Ravi asked him to speak slowly Arvind, already annoyed at the wasted morning, became upset, "Sahib, I am a certified guide, not a servant. If it were not for all the good words Surendra Ji had said about Memsahib, I would ask you to stop and let me make my way back home."

Ravi thought for a few moments before replying, "Arvind Ji, pardon me. I meant no offense. I have lived abroad for several years and have not heard much Hindi. Please be patient with me."

This apology mollified the guide and Monica's voice made him feel even better, "Yes, let us be patient and try to really listen. I want to improve my Hindi too. Theek hai, Maaji?"

Nirmala agreed wholeheartedly, "Bilkul theek hai— perfectly all right."

Arvind was pacified although he did not say a word till Ravi took a wrong turn and then the certified guide let out a torrent of words incomprehensible to everyone in the car.

The two ladies chatted, one experimenting with words and the other hoping to expand her vocabulary. Both were curious about everything they passed: mango and banyan trees providing shade to pedestrians, farmers tilling the fields with ox-ploughs, parrots and mynah birds along with sparrows and crows in the trees, herons, egrets, storks and occasional flamingos meditating in ever-deteriorating ponds. The variety of transport amused Monica the most. Along with trucks with foul smelling black exhaust, old cars held together by tape, rusty bicycles and daredevil motorcyclists, there were bicycle rickshaws, carts being pulled by thin barefoot men, horses and oxen, camels, elephants and pedestrians walking on the tarmac. They passed a village every ten miles or so with crowds of women in colourful cotton saris or lahangas and men in colourful headgear with a thick tail to cover their neck. There were stalls selling fruits, vegetables, sweets and cold lemon drinks. These were located on the dusty sidewalks between open sewers and the tarmac. Flies and wasps hovered over the food and neither the sellers nor the customers were bothered by them. Little boys and girls chased the car begging for money. Monica opened her purse to find some coins but Nirmala stopped her, "Don't give them money. Other expectant beggars will surround the car and cause a lot of trouble. We will donate to the orphanage at the temple."

This was the first time Ravi had driven in India and the progress was slow. Around noon when they were an hour away from Brindavan, the birthplace of Lord Krishna, Ravi thought his concentration was wavering. "It will be one before we get to Brindavan. We should have a rest stop to stretch our legs," He suggested.

"Are you hungry?" Nirmala asked Monica in Hindi pointing to her stomach and food.

"I am not starving but some food will be welcome all the same. Yes, we should make this stop a lunch break," Monica replied.

Ravi drove a short distance on a dirt side road and stopped. Arvind spread a mat under a banyan tree in a space between the roots. Within a few minues a crowd of about thirty onlookers, men, women and children, had gathered around them. "There is a saying that nothing grows under a banyan tree. But it seems a lot grows around it," Ravi said to Monica looking at the villagers. Arvind tried to shoo them away but Monica stopped him, "They are just watching. They are not doing any harm."

"Theek Hai memsahib. As you please. But please do not offer them any food. They are ignorant people with their silly beliefs and will not accept it from you. They do not care about hurting your feelings," Arvind's was a voice of experience.

"They are fascinated by a white woman in traditional Indian clothes. We have to get used to it. They are not unfriendly, just curious. We will have the band of followers every time we are outdoors," Ravi gave Monica a gentle warning.

"I like them. The kids are so sweet. Listening and talking to them will improve my Hindi. I much prefer it to Italy where they are always pinching your behind," Monica replied.

Nirmala served the parathas with potato and okra curries as well as yoghurt. They ate the food and washed it down with chai from the flask, paying little attention to the chatter of the crowd. The villagers dissolved in the surrounding fields when Nirmala and Monica started to pack the leftovers. The meal raised every one's spirit and Arvind became chatty again. Ravi now sensed his meaning and translated the interesting bits to Monica.

When they were back in the car, Monica asked Nirmala, "Maaji, you have lived in interesting times of so many social and political changes. You must tell me all about your life."

Nirmala looked at her innocent inquisitor and murmured, "I am a poor woman with no education. I have lived an ordinary life, just like millions of women. There is nothing I can tell that can be even remotely of interest to you."

Monica was not to be deflected by this modesty, however genuine it might have been. She changed the tack a little, "Thik hai Maaji. Then tell me all all about your pilgrimage. You must tell me the places you visited, how you traveled and where you stayed?"

Nirmala looked at the eager face of her young daughter-in-law and sighed. After some reflection she said, "I went to a lot of places all over the country. Holy places, not only for Jains but for other sects too. I took a bus or a train, whatever was cheaper. Other travelers were very kind and made room for me to sit down even when many were standing. Mostly I stayed in Dharmshalas."

Ravi was listening to the conversation and butted in, "Maaji, let me explain Dharmshala to Monica. Many temples have a lodge associated with them. It is called Dharmshala—abode of the religious. It provides simple accommodation to pilgrims on a pay what you can basis. They come in all sizes but the design is similar; a square courtyard with rooms on three sides and washrooms on the fourth side. Cooking is done in the courtyard on open wood or coal stoves. Rooms are identical, about ten feet square with doors and windows opening on the courtyard and a single 40 watt bulb hanging precariously from the ceiling. A covered verandah separates the courtyard and the rooms and provides shelter from the sun and the rain."

"I want to stay in one in Mathura" Monica said.

"There is one very good one in Chaurasi just before Mathura. It is a Jain temple, so beautiful, Memsahib must see it," Arvind informed them.

"Ok, that is what we will do. We will go there after Brindavan and go to Mathura temples tomorrow. Maaji will love to pray in the temple in the evening," Monica said turning towards Nirmala. However, dear Maaji had dozed off, "Good, a nap will help her to recoup energy for our walk around the birth place of Lord Krishna," thought Monica.

———◇◇———

Arvind guided Ravi to a less traveled side road to avoid the crowds at the Railway station and they reached the ancient jail where Lord Krishna is believed to have been born five millennia ago. "Sahib, we are lucky it is Monday afternoon. It gets really crowded at prayer times in the morning and the evening and on the Tuesdays you can wait for hours to get in. Towards the end of seventeenth century, Moghul emperor Aurangzeb destroyed some of the temples and built a mosque. Some Hindus now want to destroy the mosque and rebuild the temples. To keep these fanatics out the security is tight. That is why even a small line can take a while," Arvind informed them and whispered to Ravi as he saw a security guard approach them, "That guard is coming to take us past the line. He will be happy with the baksheesh of five rupees." Indeed, a security guard had noticed Monica, appropriately dressed in a cotton sari, and escorted the little group ahead of about a hundred or so devotees in the queue. Ravi thought, "The corruption has its uses," as he surreptitiously handed the guard a grey roll of paper.

Nirmala was energized by the holy place. "Jains have twenty-four deities of their own and do not normally worship Krishna, but I feel good in every temple," she told Monica. Deftly making a path for them through the crowd of devotees, she led them past the weathered statues of Maya Devi, mother of Buddha, to Krishna's birthplace. "The walls are exactly as they were at His birth," Nirmala said. They looked at heaps of mud, straw and gravel and courteously nodded agreement. She led them to the glorious life size statues of Krishna and his beloved Radha and smaller ones of other Hindu gods and goddesses. Nirmala said the same short prayer for every one.
"What does the prayer mean?" Monica asked Ravi.
"Maaji is expressing her devotion and asking for blessing for her family," Ravi replied. "The mosque looks dilapidated. Should we go inside and have a look?" Monica asked. This

was one wish Ravi couldn't satisfy, "We should give it a pass. Maaji's feelings might be hurt. She has tolerance for all religions but it does not extend to entering the mosque built on the site of a temple"

They heard the chant "Hare Krishna Hare Hare" in the Bhajan Kutir—hymn cottage—and saw the inscriptions from Bhagwad Gita on their way out. Then they drove to the temple of Bankey Bihari—Naughty Krishna—but it was closed for another half hour. "I don't think it is worthwhile to wait. It is another half hour to Mathura and it will be dark in an hour or so," Nirmala said thinking of her vow not to eat after dark.

Monica, realizing that Nirmala did not know the plan for the evening, said "Maaji, when you were asleep, we thought you will like to pray in the Jain temple in Chaurasi and stay in the Dharmshala there for the night. Do you agree with the plan?"

Nirmala's face lit up, "I have always wanted to go to that temple but never could. It is wonderful, really wonderful. You are an angel to think of it, Monica. I will bless you for this day till Bhagwan Mahavir calls me."

The temple was surrounded by a well kept garden and there was ample parking on both sides of the road. "Let us go to the Dharmshala and get the room. We will visit the temple later," directed Nirmala. She asked a young man dressed in a white cotton loin cloth and cotton chappals the directions to Dharmshala. "There are two, I will take you to the one which is closer. Follow me," he replied and they walked to an open window behind the complex. The young man peeked inside the window and shouted, "Daya Maharaj, are you in?" An older man dressed in white came to the window.

Nirmala leaned forward, "Four of us would like to spend the night with you here."

"This Dharmshala is for Jains only. And foreigners are not allowed to pollute the grounds of our temple."

"We are Jains. What proof do you need?"

"I have no doubt Mataji that you are a Jain. But how can that Gori be a Jain, please tell me."

"This young man is my son and the Gori is his wife. My son is a Jain and his wife is a Jain too."

"Main pooja kar sakti hoon—I can pray." Monica told the gatekeeper.

The old man relented and showed them a room. There were three string cots in the room and one on the verandah. The room had a fan, two light bulbs and a cooking area in the far corner with a small stove and a couple of empty buckets but there was no indication of any one ever having used it. The dirt floor was clean and walls were recently whitewashed. Two windows, on either side of the entrance door, had cast iron bars and opened on the verandah. No pots, pans or bedding were provided because the pilgrims traveled with their own. By now the shadows were getting long. Arvind found a coolie to bring the bags from the car. Thanks to Geeta's foresight, there was enough food left from lunch for an adequate dinner and they had it sitting on the bare cots in the courtyard surrounded by groups of other pilgrims who were also enjoying their simple dinners of chapati and vegetable curry. The mosquitoes and flies were waved away, no one tried to kill them.

After dinner Nirmala, Monica and Ravi walked over to the temple. "There were twenty four Tirthankars (Holy messengers), Adinath was the first and Mahavir the last. Ajitnath, the main deity of this temple was one of the earlier ones, I am not sure which," Nirmala told them. They took their shoes off to enter the prayer hall which could accommodate five hundred worshippers. The beautifully-sculptured white marble idol of Ajitnath was in the centre. Nine other messengers were placed around the temple. All ten faces looked the same to Monica and Ravi but they did not say it out of respect for

Nirmala. Nirmala sat down cross-legged on the floor and the young couple stood with bowed heads on either side of her. She recited a series of prayers. Then the bells chimed and a priest came forward, bowed to the idol and said a loud prayer which was enthusiastically repeated by the worshippers, Monica included.

It was pitch dark when they made their way back to their room. They walked slowly in silence, basking in the peace that had settled in their hearts.

By the time Ravi and Monica opened their eyes in the morning, Nirmala had bathed. "I will be quick with the prayers, no more than half an hour. We should leave soon after that," she told them on her way out. They leisurely sipped from earthen mugs of steaming tea Arvind had brought for them from a stall outside the temple. Now properly awake, they got out of cots and were packed and ready to leave a few minutes before Nirmala returned with a most ethereal look on her face.

When every one had settled in the car, Ravi turned the engine on and asked Arvind, "What is next?"

Arvind had his reply ready, "There are hundreds of tem ples of Krishna and his beloved Radha in Mathura and you could live for a hundred years and not be able to visit them all. We only have time for one and, if Maaji agrees, we should go to Dwarkadhish temple. It is the most popular temple with the tourists." Nirmala agreed and this two hundred year old temple became their destination in the holy city founded five thousand years ago. Arvind guided Ravi through narrow cobbled streets crowded with men and women of all ages, cows, bulls, stray mangy dogs, stalls for every thing under the sun and hawkers selling trinkets for pennies.

"The temple is quiet now but at the festival times there are great celebrations and worshippers come in huge numbers from all over the country to receive a blessing," Arvind informed them as they entered the impressive building. Monica stayed with Nirmala who prayed before the images of Radha and Krishna while Ravi walked around looking at the images of other gods and splendid carvings and paintings. When Nirmala had finished her prayer, Ravi showed Monica the carvings and remarked, "These were carved with hammer and chisel two hundred years ago but the craft goes back a thousand years. You will see outstanding examples of figures carved in stone in a couple of days that were done nine hundred years ago."

"Destination Taj Mahal," Ravi announced as they settled in the car. But Nirmala had a slightly different view, "We should go to Red Fort first, check into the hotel next and visit the Taj after dinner. It looks much better without the glare of the afternoon sun."

Arvind agreed, "Maaji is right, as always. We can also visit the Taj in the morning to see it in a different light and then set off for Fatehpur Sikri. It will make for a long day tomorrow but we can't miss the beautiful old city, can we Maaji?"

"Of course not," Nirmala put her seal of approval.

When they had left the crowds of the city behind, Monica asked Nirmala, "Maaji, what do you say in your prayer to the gods?"

"Bitiya, we sing the glory of the avatar of God, the glory of the creation, and pray that he looks after His devotees."

Monica knew that Bitiya meant beloved daughter and being recognized as one made her heart jump with joy. "Maaji, will you pray for the happiness of your son and your Bitiya too?"

"I ask for blessings and general kindness but do not pray with any specific request in mind on behalf of any particular individual. I do not recommend it. We are all His creatures and He does the best for all of us, even though we do not often appreciate it." Nirmala turned the other way while saying this but Monica did not miss the tinge of sadness in her voice she had noticed on earlier occasions.

7

"I am feeling a little tired. I will rest in the car while you go to see the fort," Nirmala said. Ravi wrapped her in a light blanket and helped her lie comfortably on the back seat. He hired a young man to watch the car. "Send some one to find us if Maaji is uncomfortable. We will return immediately. Do not disturb her in any way and do not go away whatever happens." Arvind instructed him.

"The fort was built by the Moghul emperor Shahjehan, whose son, incidentally, was Aurangzeb who destroyed temples to build mosques. It is located on the bank of river Yamuna and built mainly of red sandstone with marble used to add to the grandeur of special places. The walls are hollow and water flowed through them to keep the rooms cool," Arvind told them. He guided them through Diwan-e-Aam (Hall of Commoners), an ornate pavillion, and the emperor's palace. They looked through the window at Taj Mahal gleaming across the wide river just as the aging Shahjehan must have done when he was the prisoner of Aurangzeb and shared some of the grief the emperor had to endure in his dying days. On the way back, Monica told Ravi of the joy she felt when Nirmala called her Bitiya and her sadness following their conversation. "You have won her over. But she can't let go of her son. It is very sad. I feel so guilty for breaking my word." Monica felt a sharp twist in her heart but thought it wise to let it pass and suppressed her response.

Arvind guided them to a modest hotel with a vegetarian restaurant. After settling in their room Nirmala lay down on the bed and said, "The young lovers should see the everlasting symbol of love by themselves. I have seen it a number of times and I need rest more than any thing else. We have another long day tomorrow."

"Maaji, you look tired and a nice sleep is what you need. Let me help you get to sleep," Monica agreed. She brought her a glass of water for her medicines while Ravi messaged her arms, shoulders and feet. "Just like the times you were a young boy," Nirmala whispered as she closed her eyes.

They saw the miracle built out of white marble, spotless like the love of the emperor for his Mumtaz, the incredible tapestry of precious stones inlaid in white marble and amazing marble screens around the cenotaphs of the emperor and the empress. While admiring the worldly expression of the beauty of love, Monica and Ravi felt their own love ascending to a new level.

Monica and Ravi returned to see the grandeur of Taj in a different light the next morning. They took their time going round the dome holding hands and admiring the view of the river and the fort on the other bank. Arvind decided that it was best not to rush them. It was noon when they reached Fatehpur Sikri. "This is the beautiful, deserted capital city of the Mughals and was built by Emperor Akbar, grandfather of Shahjehan, in the late 16th century. The city was built in honour of the great Sufi saint Sheikh Salim Chisti after whose blessings a childless Akbar got an heir, naturally named Salim. We will only have time to visit the tomb of Salim Chisti, red sandstone structures of the Jama Masjid, the five storey palace Panch Mahal and the Palace of Queen Jodha Bai. She was a Rajput princess. Akbar wished to improve relations among Hindus and Muslims by marrying princesses from different communities. That is why the structures in this city reflect a blend of Islamic, Hindu and Persian styles of architecture" Arvind said by way of introduction. He was not a man of few words.

"When did the capital move to Agra?" Monica asked.

"Akbar did not stay here very long; the city ran out of water or something catastrophic like that. He moved the capital to Lahore to scare away the invaders from the West. Later the capital moved to Delhi again before Shahjehan moved it to Agra," Arvind replied.

"Emperors liked to move their capital in those days; sometimes there were good reasons but mostly it was self-aggrandisement," Ravi added.

The pilgrimage with Nirmala was having an unforeseen effect, it was deepening the love between the young couple by giving Monica an understanding of the cultural and family background of her husband who, in turn, was developing a new awareness of his wife's emotional maturity.

8

It was a four hour drive to Jaipur including the short stop for chai and pakoras from a roadside stall. Arvind guided them to a Rajasthan Tourist Board hotel near the Hawa Mahal, a tourist destination in the centre of the city. The place was clean and reasonably priced. Here too the restaurant was a vegetarian establishment acceptable to Nirmala. After dinner, Nirmala visited a temple nearby and Monica and Ravi went for a walk in the crowded bazaar. Monica attracted attention of men and women who stared at her unabashedly but moved over so the couple could stroll at their own pace. The shop keepers shouted to her, "Memsahib. Have chai with us while looking at the rare items I have collected from all over India," or whatever they thought would attract her attention. But they disregarded the invitations remembering Nirmala's advice, "Look at the shops but don't buy anything. They will rob you blind."

Monica had something more important to discuss with Ravi. "You haven't noticed how ill Maaji is. She is putting up a brave face for your sake but she is completely drained."

"I hadn't noticed anything unusual. She never looked particularly strong. The doctor said that she was doing just fine."

"Listen to me just this time please. She is not long for this world. Spend as much time with her as possible. You are not going to see her again."

"I hope to see her many more times but I will spend more time with her. We will reduce our social engagements to a minimum and I will stay by her side. You should ask her about her life and how she coped with all her misfortunes."

"I only want her to think of good times in our few days together. So you talk to her about those. I will be there to listen. You are her son, the favourite one from all appearances. You have to make this a good memory for her."

"I see your point. I will do my best. She has been a wonderful mother and in no way can I repay her for what she has done for me."

Nirmala was in bed when they returned. She was staring at the ceiling breathing normally. Ravi sat down at the edge facing her and held both her hands in his. "Maaji, you do not look well. Is all this travel too much for you?"

"I travelled much bigger distances in rickety buses. This car is a luxury for me. and Monica looks after me like an angel. Don't worry about me. You enjoy yourself and give your bride a good impression of the country.And who knows when you will come again? It is far and it costs a lot."

"Maaji, I will come to see you every year. I will send you five hundred rupees every month. You do whatever you fancy with the money. If you need more, just drop me a note. Monica and I want your remaining years to be happy and will contribute as much as is within our means. You do not need to go without anything you wish for yourself or any one else."

"You know what will make me happy but you can't do it now. All this money talk is a consolation prize. I am too old and too weak to fight for what is my due. I am a beggar now. Give me what you can spare and I will make do with it."

Ravi wiped the droplets in the corners of her eyes with the end of her sari. "Maaji, you are not well. I will call a doctor. We need to decide whether to go back home or carry on."

"I am not going home till I have been to the temple in Mount Abu. I am tired, not ill. The burdens of the past, even more the disappointments, are weighing me down. I will be better in the morning. You can call the doctor then if I don't improve."

Nirmala did seem better after the night's sleep. She had a bath in cold water, dressed and prepared to leave. Ravi knew she was going to the temple but Monica was alarmed, "Maaji where are you going so early without any breakfast?"

Nirmala replied in a soft tone, "I feel the need to pray. I will spend the morning in the temple while you go sight seeing. We will meet here at noon to make plans for the afternoon. It will give you enough time to see Amber palace."

"Maaji, Ravi has seen the palace several times. He will go with you to the temple. I will go with Arvind to the palace in a taxi with Arvind."

"That is a good idea," Ravi agreed and added, "The elephant ride from where the taxi leaves you to the gate on top of the hill is a lot of fun and make sure Arvind takes you to the hall of mirrors," Ravi said They had a quick breakfast of parathas, yoghurt and mixed vegetable curry with chai and went their separate ways.

9

Nirmala felt a thrill when Ravi prayed along with her. As a child he visited the temples rarely and with great reluctance. However, he seemed to remember most of the verses which he was reciting with gusto in a pleasant baritone. But a lot of his prayer was done silently standing in front of the idol with hands folded and eyes shut. Nirmala suspected that he was asking for the forgiveness for the grief he has caused his mother and praying for her recovery while she was praying for his happiness wherever Bhagwan wished him to live.

After the prayer Nirmala said to Ravi, "I am feeling well but I think a rest in the afternoon will do me good. You should show Monica the sights in the city while I regain some of my energy."

"Maaji, you are looking better than you have on this trip. But do rest," Ravi agreed. Monica and Ravi went to the Hawa Mahal, the palace of windows, Jantar Mantar—largest stone and marble crafted observatory in the world and saw all seventeen sundials—and walked around the crowded bazaar to absorb the spirit of the historic "Pink city."

They found Nirmala in good spirits when they returned. "That nap did wonders for me. I am ready to go to temple after dinner. Does any one want to come with me?"

"I will come to the temple with you. The worries of this world seem to wash away when I am in the temple even though I do not understand the words of the prayers," Monica answered.

"I will come too. I can explain the prayers to our convert here," Ravi said patting Monica's back.

"I am glad both of you are coming with me. We can say a prayer for his Pitaji who would have been fifty five today."

"Maaji, you still remember Pitaji fondly although he did not look after the family," Monica said with the intonation of a query.

Nirmala's eyes moistened a little, "He was a very good husband." She paused to collect herself and continued, "He never raised his voice in anger with me. He always had good things to say about his family, in private and in public, even though the sons were often rude and said cruel things to him. His problem was that he couldn't take on any job because he was so scared of doing it wrong. It must have something to do with a dominant father and an alcoholic mother who doted on him when she was sober and screamed at him when drunk. Such an upbringing would ruin any one. His brother was no great shakes either; left home to do a lowly clerical job at the railway station. I told him not to look for menial jobs which would lower the family and make it harder for the sons. I insisted on marrying him when I was a child of fourteen and did not know anything about life. But I have never regretted it. He respected me for what I was and gave me the sons who would make any mother proud. Our private life was wonderful from the wedding night to his last days. When we were alone he made me feel like an empress even when my sari had holes in it. I have missed him every moment of my day since he left. He would have been so proud to see Ravi do so well in England and happy that he found such a good wife."

"Maaji, Ravi is learning. We both realise that the words are arrows; once you have sent them they can't be recalled. I am so sorry that I never met Pitaji."

"Satya and Ravi look just like him except that they are about four inches shorter. He was the tallest and handsomest man in any group when I met him. Unfortunately, the anxiety about family's finances and his inability to do anything about it gnawed at his innards and he looked old much before his time. But he bore it by himself. No one heard him complain about his fate or blame any one but himself for our misfortunes."

10

They reached Mount Abu a little after ten the next morning. They drove rapidly past the beautiful Nakhi Lake reflecting Aravalli hills in all their splendour in their rush to get to Dilwara temple in time reserved for the worshippers of Jain faith when tourists are not allowed entry. The guard showed some hesitation before letting Monica in but once again her Hindi words persuaded him to let them pass. They entered the grounds through a narrow entrance, main gate being closed to keep the hordes of tourist out. There are two temples, one for each of the two Jain sects, Shwetamber—white clad and Digamber—sky clad. The family belonged to the second sect but only the monks practised the sky clad—no clothes—part of the religion. Nirmala always wore white as did the worshippers when praying, either in the temple or in the shrine at home. "The temples were built between eleventh and thirteenth centuries by the Finance Ministers of Maharaja of Mewar at a cost of five hundred million dollars in today's currency," Nirmala told them and added, "Even the non-believers come from far and wide to admire the fine marble sculptures and carvings. "I am heading to the temples to pray, you look around and meet me at the Digambar temple when you finish."

Monica and Ravi took their time walking around the vast compound with numerous buildings in addition to the temples. The architecture, carved windows and door frames, statues of humans and animals were impressive but particularly outstanding were the forty images of twenty-four holy messengers, some repeated. These were located in little alcoves in the walls of four verandahs around a courtyard. Each image was beautifully chiseled from white marble, showing messengers in meditation seated in a lotus pose—legs crossed such that feet were almost touching the hips—peace and wisdom radiating from their faces.

No sooner had they joined Nirmala, they were swallowed by the waves of visitors who had rushed in as soon as the gates opened. However, in consideration for a Gori, the crowd parted just enough to let them out unjostled.

The sun was blazing hot when they came out of the temple. Arvind guided them to a restaurant which would be acceptable to Nirmala's religious scruples and served good food. They split up for the afternoon. Arvind escorted Nirmala to the temples of Adhar Devi and Shri Raghunathji while Monica and Ravi went for a boat ride on heavenly Nakhi Lake dug in prehistoric times by gods with their nakhs, nails, hence the name. In the evening they walked up to the Sunset Point, trailed as usual by a huge crowd of followers fascinated by a sari-clad young gori who could speak Hindi. While waiting for the sunset at the top of the hill, visitors insisted on including Monica in their family photographs and recorded her broken Hindi on their videos. Then, without any notice the sky darkened noticeably and everyone turned towards the West to witness in total silence a huge red ball slowly sinking behind the thickly-forested valley.

11

The drive to Udaipur was uneventful. As they approached the airport Arvind remarked, "Funny isn't it? If the plane is late, as it always is, sometimes by 24 hours, you wait. But if you are late even by a few minutes they sell your seat and fly away leaving you in the lurch." But for once the plane from Mumbai was on time. The driver to take the car and Arvind back was waiting for them. They checked in for two window and one aisle seats. "Maaji, it is your first time in the air. I know how exciting it is. You should take the window seat. I will sit next to you and you can tell me what you see. Ravi can sit with the stranger in the other window seat," Monica said with the authority of a considerate daughter-in-law.

Nirmala appeared calm as they walked on the hot tarmac to the plane. Ravi supported his mother on the stairs to the plane and helped her with the seat belt. Monica settled herself and held her mother-in-law's hand. It was tiny, brown rough skin on soft bones. She felt once more that Nirmala was not long for this world and a sadness came over her. Nirmala noticed the change in mood, put her other hand on

Monica's cheek and asked, "What happened? You look as if you are holding back tears."

"Maaji, I have been so happy in my short stay with you. You and every one else have been so kind to me. Soon we will leave and this visit will be a memory. All of us need you and you look so weak. I am so afraid for you."

"Whatever Bhagwan wishes happens. And it always turns out to be good in the end, however bad it looks at the moment. Smile and enjoy the time you are allowed. I will always pray for you."

Nirmala gripped Monica's arm a as the plane sped up. The grip relaxed when the plane left the ground. Ravi called across the isle, "Maaji, we are flying."

"Look at the Maharaja's palace in the lake. It looks so tiny from the air, and so beautiful," Nirmala said pointing to the scene in the distance. "The buildings look just like match boxes, cars crawling like ants, can't even see any people," she continued.

Nirmala did not take her eyes away from the window for a moment, not even when the landscape stayed the same arid semidesert for long stretches. She refused the airline meal, "Cooked and handled by who knows who?" she said. It turned out to be quite good and Ravi was glad to have her plate too. She did take a short break—to gulp down the pills Monica gave her with the water they had brought with them. Ravi watched his mother's exhilaration with amusement and derived some satisfaction in having been able to provide her a novel experience.

12
—◇◇—

Other than a hurried visit to Naniji, much of the rest of their stay in India was spent at home with Nirmala and in entertaining relatives who showered Monica with expensive gifts. When it came time to pack, she had to find room for a multitude of silk saris in gorgeous colours, and lengths of materials for blouses and petticoats to match, jewellery to wear for fancy occasions, and ornaments to decorate the home. "We would have had to charter a ship, if we had got married here," she said to Ravi and added "Why did you not suggest it?

"Your parents were suspicious enough already. Such a suggestion would have sent them overboard" Ravi replied somewhat shamefaced.

Their flight was at midnight. Nirmala emphatically turned down Monica's request to accompany her to the temple. She must have prayed long and hard because Satya and Geeta were getting worried about her. She arrived at last, loaded with bags of fruits and local sweets. "Fruit for Monica and sweets for Ravi; they will need sustainance on the long flight," she said handing them to Geeta for packaging.

"Maaji, these will last for weeks. The flight is only a few hours," Ravi pointed out when he looked at the bags.

"You can finish them when you get home. They will last." Geeta tactfully supported her mother-in-law.

The afternoon was a busy time with older visitors dropping by to bless their Gori bahu and younger ones to compliment Ravi, albeit with a little envy, on his good fortune. Monica got good exercise bending down to touch so many feet. Geeta had anticipated the flow of traffic and prepared for it. Chai and mango juice flowed freely with samosas, jalebis, gulab jamuns and other delicacies. The visitors in the evening stayed for the dinner of chapatis, rice, potato and cauliflower curries and lentil daal. There was a sense of relief when the last visitor left about an hour before they were due to leave for the airport. They slumped on chairs which had been arranged along the walls in anticipation of the visitors. Satya poured himself a scotch and Geeta heated milk for Monica and Ravi. A sense of melancholy now pervaded the room and no one seemed to know what to say. After a while Ravi broke the silence, "Bhaiya and Bhabi, I must say this on behalf of Monica and myself: you have been absolutely fabulous the way you have looked after Maaji. She is recovering quite nicely. This little trip was very tiring for her but it probably did her some good." Ravi took Nirmala's hand in his and added, "Now you must make sure that she doesn't go on another tiring pilgrimage before she is fully recovered. Bhabi, she will listen to you more than to any one else so it is your primary responsibility."

Geeta was flattered but not fooled, "Bhaiya, you are always saying kind things. The person Maaji listens to is you. You better tell her directly what she should or should not do."

Ravi applied gentle pressure on Nirmala's hand, turned to face her and said, "Maaji, your health is improving but you are not young any more. You need to spend your time in prayer at home, or in the local temple, not on pilgimmages. Monica and I will look after the money part and Bhaiya and Bhabi will take care of every thing else. We will visit you as often as we can. Both Bhaiyas and Bhabis need you to guide them and your grandchildren. Your advice is always being sought in the community. People here need you. They really do."

The silence returned to the room for a long minute. Then Nirmala responded, "I will stay where I am welcome and for as long as I am welcome. When I become a burden, I will find a corner in a Dharmshala and spend the rest of my days in prayer. I appreciate what you are offering me and I assure you it will be used for good causes."

Monica had her say at last, "Maaji, your blessing means more to me than all the treasures of the world. Say a word for us too in your prayers, please."

Nirmala's eyes moistened and she whispered, "I prayed for Ravi to return after two years. Bhagwan had another course for him and turned my request down. Then I prayed for his well-being. This time He listened and sent the goddess

Saraswati herself to look after him. Now I will pray that He gives Ravi enough sense to realize his good fortune and become worthy of her." Nirmala folded her hands, looked upwards and said in a clear tone, "Bhagwan, grant this, my last request."

13

Next morning, Geeta found Nirmala lying still on her string bed wrapped in the tartan blanket, her face calm, body cold and lifeless.